The Club Trilogy book two

THE RECLAMATION

Lauren Rowe

The Reclamation Copyright © 2015

Published by SoCoRo Publishing
Layout by www.formatting4U.com
Cover design © Sarah Hansen, Okay Creations LLC

Dedication

To B, S and C for teaching me every day about deep and abiding love.

Chapter 1
Jonas

There are two twitching, trembling women standing in my living room right now—and I'm not talking about the good kind of twitching, trembling women. Sarah and Kat are scared shitless right now, freaking out about their places being ransacked and their computers stolen (undoubtedly by the motherfuckers at The Club), and wondering if today's events represent the sum total of the iceberg slamming into them or just the tip of it. And I can't blame them for being scared. Now that Sarah knows the truth about The Club—and The Club *knows* she knows their secret—what might those fuckers be willing to do to protect their global cash-cow-prostitution-ring? Well, I'm not going to wait to find out. I'm taking these motherfuckers down.

I admit I don't have the slightest idea *how* I'm going to take them down at the moment, but whatever I come up with, it's going to be definitive, unequivocal, and effective. End of story. Or, at least, I hope so.

Fuck.

To be honest, I don't think I can do this on my own—I'm definitely not used to wearing a red cape—but when my brother gets here and the two of us put our Wonder Twin powers together, when we combine my brain with Josh's sheer awesomeness, and then throw Josh's hacker friend into the mix, whoever he is, we'll be unstoppable. I know we will.

We'd better be.

How did everything get so fucked up? Only an hour ago, Sarah and I were floating on cloud nine after arriving home from our magical trip to Belize—the two of us gliding up the walkway to her

5

apartment, high on each other and on life, having experienced every form of ecstasy known to man over the past four days. We climbed waterfalls in Belize and leaped into dark chasms and toppled Mount Everest again and again and again and again in our tree-house-cocoon built for two, all the while discovering, with astonishing force and clarity, that the two of us were innately designed for each other in every conceivable way.

Being with Sarah down there in Belize, I felt... I get shivers even thinking about how I felt... I felt *happy,* genuinely *happy,* for the first time in my whole life—or, at least, for the first time since I was seven years old.

Holding Sarah's naked body against mine all night long, touching every inch of her, looking into her big brown eyes as I made love to her again and again, sitting on the deck of the tree house and holding her hand while listening to the jungle all around us, talking with her for hours and hours about everything and nothing and laughing 'til my sides hurt, getting my ass kicked by her every which way, telling her the things I've never told anyone before—even the things I'm ashamed of—just sitting there, mesmerized, watching her eat a fucking mango—it didn't matter what we were doing, that woman made me start believing in rainbows and unicorns and even the crown jewel of Valentine's Day bullshit—happily ever afters. (Really, I should just mail my Man Card to the fuckers at Hallmark and Lifetime with a note that says, "You win, motherfuckers.") What Sarah and I experienced down there in Belize was nothing short of the ideal realm, precisely as Plato described it.

And then, boom, we got back to Seattle and the shit hit the fan. Sarah's place was trashed and her computer stolen. And now she's scared out of her mind, understandably, and I'm standing here like a jackass, my mouth agape, trying desperately to figure out—*What would Superman do?*

I need a foolproof strategy for decimating The Club—and I swear I'm going to come up with one the minute Josh gets here, I really am— but right now I'm just too amped up to think straight on my own. Left to my own devices, all I can think about is wrapping my arms around Sarah and making love to her, tenderly, purposefully, ardently, and whispering "I love you" into her ear as I do it.

I had my chance to say those three little words to her in the limo on the way over here, but, pussy-ass that I am, I didn't seize the opportunity. I wanted to do it, but we were on our way to pick up Kat, and my heart was pounding in my ears, and I wanted to say the words and *show* her at the same time. And then, two minutes later, Kat hopped into the backseat of the limo with us and the two of them started clutching each other and sobbing and the moment went up in smoke.

Okay, fine, yes, fuck me, I blew it. I know I did. I should have told her.

And now we're here in my house—with Kat in tow, of course—and I'm standing here with my usual hard-on for Sarah and my thumb up my ass. I can't stop thinking about making love to her and whispering those three little words into her ear as I do it—and yet I'm mad at myself for even thinking about that right now. Quite obviously, sex is the last thing on Sarah's mind, and I don't blame her. She's scared and worried and frazzled and freaking out, as any sane person would be. What she needs right now, obviously, is a strong man who's going to make her feel safe and protected—not an asshole who's going to keep poking her in the hip with his inexhaustible hard-on. Seriously. But I can't help myself. She just turns me on, no matter the circumstances, even when all hell's breaking loose.

I look over at the ladies. They've moved to the couch, and they're talking softly to each other. Sarah looks on edge. Kat's got her arm around Sarah's shoulders, reassuring her. The two of them look completely exhausted—especially Sarah, who spent all day traveling only to come home to a wrecked apartment.

Looking at the anguish on her beautiful face as she talks to Kat, it's all the more clear I'm a total asshole for thinking what I'm thinking. I need to rein myself in and focus on taking care of her. What I need to do is divorce my mind from my insatiable body. I need to aspire to my best self—the ideal form of Jonas Faraday. I need to visualize the divine original. Yes. *Visualize the divine original.* I take a deep breath. *Visualize the divine original.*

"Can I get you girls anything?" I ask feebly. "Something to eat or drink?"

Sarah shakes her head and opens her mouth to speak.

"You got any tequila?" Kat asks.

I smirk. Sarah's told me all about Best Friend Kat.

"I don't know what I've got in the house," I reply to Kat. "I'll look." I never drink tequila, but Josh loves it. I'm sure he's left a bottle around here somewhere.

I glance at Sarah.

She flashes me a wan smile—but even when she's tired, her eyes are full of warmth. But, wait, is there something else twinkling behind those big brown eyes besides warmth? Is that *heat*?

I try to grin at her, but I'm too jacked up to smile. I can feel my mouth twitching, so I look away. I wish we were alone, just the two of us. I wish this craziness with The Club weren't hanging over us. I wish we were still in Belize.

I head to the kitchen to look for whatever booze Josh might have graced me with on one of his many visits. Bingo. There's a big bottle of Gran Patron in a corner cabinet. I should have known—only the best for Josh.

I rummage around for shot glasses.

I hear Sarah and Kat murmuring softly to each other in the living room. Their voices sound anxious, on edge. Sarah's obviously scared and worried—and nothing else. Yeah, I was definitely imagining that heat in her eyes, probably just wishing it were there. I need to think about what she needs right now and stop thinking about what I want—what I always want. Sarah deserves nothing less.

This whole situation is a giant cluster fuck, I swear to God. Why, oh why did I join The Club? Why, oh why did I fuck Stacy the Faker—or should I say Stacy the Prostitute? Jesus. Why, oh why didn't I let Sarah take her computer to Belize like she wanted to? And why, oh why, oh why didn't I listen to Sarah's intuition?

From day one, even before Stacy accosted Sarah in that sports bar bathroom, Sarah told me, "I keep feeling like there's got to be some sort of consequence for what I've done," as if contacting me against The Club's rules was some sort of mortal sin. "You didn't defy *The Church*," I scoffed, misreading the situation completely. Why didn't I take a step back and really listen to her? She's so damned smart, I should have known to take her seriously, no matter what. If I'd only listened to her, instead of swinging my dick around and acting like I know everything like I always do, maybe none of this would have happened. In so many ways, I've totally blown it here. And now it's up to me to make things right.

I can't find any shot glasses. Juice glasses will have to do. I look in my fridge for a lime. Nope. I pour three double shots of Patron and head back into the living room with a shaker of salt.

I hand the ladies their drinks. "No limes," I say. "Sorry."

"Cheers," Kat says, taking a glass and the shaker of salt from me. "To you, Jonas. Thanks for the hospitality." She raises her glass. "Nice to meet you, by the way."

"Nice to meet you, too. You're everything Sarah said you'd be."

Sarah smirks at me. She knows exactly how she described Kat— "a party girl with a heart of gold."

I clink my drink with Kat's. "Sorry we had to meet like this," I say.

"Yeah, well, at least this time I'm actually meeting you instead of just spying on you in a bar... " She stops. Insert foot in mouth.

I shift my weight and exhale. Wonderful. Yes, Kat, I fucked Stacy-the-Faker-Miss-Purple-Who-Turned-Out-To-Be-A-Fucking-Prostitute the night you and Sarah spied on me at The Pine Box. Nice of you to remind me of that most unpleasant fact—right in front of my girlfriend—as you sit on my couch, drinking my premium tequila.

I scrutinize Sarah's face for signs of humiliation, hurt, or embarrassment, but I don't see any of that. At least I don't think so.

Kat's face flushes bright crimson. "Sorry," she mumbles.

Sarah puts her hand on Kat's arm. "It's okay." She looks at me pointedly. "I don't give a rat's ass about any of that." She shrugs. "I really don't."

Ah, My Magnificent Sarah.

From day one, I asked Sarah if she could just forget the long (looooong) parade of women I've slept with, as well as the year's worth of purple playmates I signed up for in The Club, and she said yes. And she's never once wavered on that agreement. Not once. Because my Sarah's not like anybody else.

Kat whispers something in Sarah's ear. Sarah grins and nods.

Nothing against Kat personally, but why, oh why is she here? I want to rip Sarah's clothes off and make love to her right where she's sitting on my couch. But there's goddamned Kat, sitting there looking at me like she's laughing at me with her eyes the same way my fucking brother does.

"Bottoms up," Kat says. She licks salt off her hand and then knocks back her drink. "Good stuff." She purses her lips and exhales.

I follow suit. Surprisingly smooth. I never drink tequila. It's better than I remember it.

Sarah doesn't knock back her drink. She watches me intensely, like a cat.

Something in her eyes makes me tingle—I don't think I'm imagining that come-hither stare.

"You gonna drink that or what?" Kat says to Sarah, nudging her shoulder.

Not taking her eyes off me, Sarah shakes some salt onto her hand and then slowly, oh so slowly, licks it off with the full expanse of her tongue. She brings the rim of her glass to her beautiful lips and drinks the entire double shot in one fluid motion without so much as wincing. When she brings her head back up, she licks her lips slowly, smirking like the smart-ass she is, her eyes fixed on me.

Holy shit. I'm hard. I've never seen her do a shot before. The way she just swallowed that tequila was so sexy—so *sexual*—I'd give anything to be that tequila right now. Or maybe the rim of her glass. Or, no, wait, the *salt*. Yes, definitely the salt.

She puts her empty glass on the coffee table, leans back on the couch, and puts her hands behind her head. It's a total alpha-male move—the kind of pose a fucking CEO would strike during a hard-nosed negotiation—and it turns me on. She hasn't taken her eyes off me.

I return her smolder.

One side of her mouth hitches up.

Oh yeah, it's on. *It's on like Donkey Kong,* as Sarah would say.

"When will Josh be here?" Kat asks, yet again annoying me with her presence.

"Probably in about three hours," I say, looking at my watch. "His flight just left LAX."

Sarah sighs deeply. Her eyes are like laser beams on me, even though she's speaking to Kat. "Are you tired, Kat?"

My body is electrified. There's no way I'm imagining that look on Sarah's face right now.

Kat shakes her head and begins to speak, but Sarah cuts her off.

"Because I'm *really* tired." She looks like she wants to eat me alive. "I think I'm going to take a nice, hot shower and crawl into bed for just a bit before Josh gets here."

"Oh yeah," Kat says. "I forgot you guys have been traveling all day. You must be exhausted."

Sarah stands. Her gaze on me is relentless. "You've got a room for Kat?"

"Of course. You want me to show you now, Kat? Or do you need to eat something first?"

Sarah sighs audibly and scowls at me. She puts her hands on her hips.

Oh, shit. That last part about offering Kat food was stupid. I'm so bad at this.

"Actually, yeah, I'm—" Kat begins. But Sarah cuts her off.

"Why don't you show Kat to her room *now*. We'll eat in a bit. Is that okay with you, Kat?" Sarah turns her smoldering stare onto Kat and raises her eyebrows pointedly.

Kat raises her eyebrows, too, clearly surprised by the intensity of Sarah's gaze. "Um, sure," Kat says, slowly. When Sarah remains stone-faced, Kat's face suddenly illuminates with understanding. She smiles broadly. "Oh." Kat stands. "Yeah, of course. I'll just help myself to some fruit or crackers or whatever I can find in the kitchen to tide me over. You two go right ahead and get some... *rest*." She says the word "rest" like she's telling the punch line to a joke.

"If you're really starving I could—"

"Oh, for the love of Pete," Sarah huffs. She's pissed. "I've got mosquito repellant and airplane grime all over me." There's an undeniable edge in her voice. "I want to take a long, hot shower, Jonas Faraday. Do you understand me? A very long, *hot* shower—*right now*."

Kat laughs. "Jonas, you aren't normally this dense, are you?"

I feel myself blushing.

"He's usually not, I swear. He's actually pretty smart," Sarah says, rolling her eyes.

"If you say so."

My cheeks are hot. This is why I hate parties. This is why I hate threesomes. This is why I hate crowds. This is why I'm only good at one-on-one interactions. I flash Sarah an apologetic look, but she's not having it. She's glaring at me.

I clear my throat. "Come on, Kat." I pick up her suitcase. "I've got a perfect room for you on the other side of the house—plenty of privacy over there."

"Wonderful," Sarah says, unmistakably chastising me. She flashes a look that makes Kat giggle, and then she beelines out of the living room toward my bedroom without so much as a backward glance.

"Come on, Jonas," Kat says. "I fear for your physical safety if you keep that woman waiting any longer than necessary."

Chapter 2
Jonas

I'm standing in the doorway to Kat's room, trying my damnedest to unclench my jaw and avoid having a fucking stroke. All I want to do is go to Sarah. My body is on fire as I imagine what she might be doing right now in my bedroom—without me—but fuck me, I'm just not wired to be rude to a woman, no matter the situation. And, anyway, it's not Kat's fault she's here—it's mine. I'm the one to blame for this mess, not her.

I've made sure Kat has clean towels in her bathroom. I've told her my house is hers—whatever she wants, feel free to get it, no need to ask. In fact, please don't ask. I've showed her how to use the TV remote because it's kind of tricky. I've told her how to log in as a guest on the computer in my office to check her emails or whatever, seeing as how her laptop was stolen like Sarah's—a thought which makes me ask Kat what kind of laptop she had and quickly tap out a covert text to my assistant, directing her to buy two new laptops and have them hand-delivered to my house first thing tomorrow morning.

"So, you're good?" I ask, my heart thumping in my ears.

"I'm great. Go on. With each additional minute you keep Sarah waiting, you're putting yourself in greater and greater peril." She laughs.

I don't reply. I simply turn on my heel and dart away.

"May God be with you," she shouts to my back.

I tear through my living room toward my bedroom at the other end of the house, my hard-on raging and my heart racing. I'm going to make love to the only woman I've ever loved, nice and slow, and while I do it, I'm going to whisper, "I love you, Sarah" to her, over and over. I'm going to revel in her perfection, glory in her deliciousness—and when she comes (which is something she's gotten quite good at doing lately, I must say), I'm going to say it then, too, maybe even while I'm coming right along with her. That's definitely something I've never experienced before. Talk about a holy grail—a brand new holy grail.

Women have said those three little words to me—several women, in fact—but I've never said them back. In fact, my whole life, I've dreaded those words, avoided them like the plague—mostly because they've wound up torpedoing every goddamned relationship I've ever had, not to mention several extended flings, too. What woman is willing to say those words out loud to a man and never hear them back? It turns out, not a single one. Even if she's determined to be patient at first, to act like Mother Theresa and wait me out, the end is inevitable, if not instant, once she lets the I-love-you cat out of the bag. No relationship can last very long, if at all, when it's suddenly crystal clear only one person's heart is on the line.

But, holy fuck, I want to say those words now. And I want Sarah to say them back to me. What will it feel like to exchange those most sacred and bare words with someone? Well, not just with *someone*—with Sarah?

I can't wait.

But hang on. Wait a minute. I have a thought that stops me dead in my tracks in my hallway. What if Sarah *doesn't* say those words back to me? My stomach somersaults at the thought. What if . . .?

No, I can't think that way. We told each how we feel in Belize. *Love is a serious mental disease,* I said. And then I told her she drives me fucking crazy. You can't get much clearer than that. And then she said it back to me. *You drive me fucking crazy, too,* she said. *Loca. Cuckoo for Cocoa Puffs.*

And on top of all that I played her the Muse song, too. I've never played that Muse song for anyone before, let alone for the woman I love while making her come for the first time in her life. Oh man, that was epic. *Madness.*

I'm rock hard right now.

Yeah, we've definitely said it. *Madness.*

And now we'll take the next step. Together. We'll say the actual words . . .

But wait. What if she's scared of the magic words? Or not ready? What if she's not completely sure . . .?

14

No, no, no, I can't think that way. That's just my demons talking. That's my "deep-seated fear of abandonment wrought by childhood trauma" talking, as my therapist always explained it to me when my darkness started fucking with me and whispering in my ear. That's the crazy-ass part of me I've got to constantly guard against, push down, snuff out. I know she loves me. And I love her. I know that as surely as I know my own name. I can't let my mind run away from me.

Or my body, for that matter. For the love of God, I've got to control myself—remember she's exhausted and vulnerable and distressed right now. That she's been through a trauma today. I have to be gentle and take things slow. I have to make sure she feels safe and loved—yes, *loved*, above all else. I want to make this memorable and beautiful for her. For both of us. I have to do this just right. I can't turn into the Incredible Hulk on her right now. I have to treat her with kid gloves and make her feel safe and adored. *Worshipped.* To begin with, I'm going to pepper her face with soft kisses, the way she always does for me. And when I do, I'll tell her, *"Love is the joy of the good, the wonder of the wise, the amazement of the gods."*

I open my bedroom door, trembling with excited anticipation.

She's not in the room but I hear the shower running in my bathroom. Her clothes are strewn across the floor, leading quite explicitly into my bathroom. My heart pounds in my chest, crashes in my ears. Damn, this woman turns me on. I rip my clothes off and hurl them across the room. I head toward the bathroom.

I open my bathroom door.

She's in the shower, facing away from me, scrubbing herself with a washcloth as hot water cascades down her naked body. Her backside is pink and slick from the scalding water, her dark hair soaking wet and hanging down her back. Suds float like graceful snowflakes down the small of her back and over her beautiful, round ass. I stand for a moment, just watching her, beholding her breathtaking beauty. She's *woman-ness* personified, the perfect form of woman from the ideal realm, delivered unto the physical world as a gift for the broken and imperfect masses in order to inspire hope and aspiration—well, and to turn me the fuck on.

And she's mine, all mine. Mine, mine, mine.

She turns around and sees me. She smiles. "Talk about not taking a hint. Jeez. I've been wanting you inside me all day long, big boy."

15

I beam at her, but I don't move. She's so damned beautiful. I'm enjoying watching her.

She tilts her head to the side, letting the water wash over her. She sweeps the washcloth over her breasts.

I just keep smiling at her. She's perfect. I want to remember this moment. I love her. And I'm going to tell her so.

She puts the washcloth on the ledge and runs her bare hands over her hips and belly. She licks her lips. "Well? Are you gonna get in here or what?"

I smile. "I'm just enjoying watching you for a minute, baby. I want to remember this moment."

"Aw, how sweet," she says, but she's clearly being sarcastic. "Don't you know not to make a horny woman wait?"

I bound into the shower. "Words to live by." I take her slick body in my arms. "Say that again.'" I lean in to kiss her.

She laughs that gravelly laugh of hers. "Horny," she says, pressing her lips into mine.

I run my hands over her smooth back, down her ass, over her hips.

"I've been trying to get into your pants for the last hour, Jonas Faraday. Sometimes you really are just a big dummy, you know that?"

I kiss her mouth softly, and then I kiss her entire face, the way she always does for me—but it's not the same when water is pelting our faces. I want to whisper my devotion into her ear, but the shower stream is smacking me in the face.

I want to make her feel safe and protected . . .

She grabs my shaft and begins fondling me with enthusiasm. "Jonas, come on. I've been hot for you all day. Fuck me."

Fuck me? Wow, we're really not on the same page here. I thought she was distraught and needed something gentle and tender and beautiful . . .

"Come on," she says again. Her hands are working their magic on me. I moan.

She lifts her leg onto the shower ledge and guides me into her, then leaps up, into my arms, taking me into her. Immediately, she begins gyrating and sliding against my wet skin.

What the hell? What happened to my damsel in distress?

She throws her head back with abandon. "You feel so good," she groans out, relieved. She's on fire.

"I don't come 'til you do," I mutter.

"Oh, not that again," she moans. "Just don't talk."

She wraps her legs around my back, gyrating, writhing, slithering around in my arms. "Oh, God," she says. "Jonas." She thrusts and jerks in my arms like an animal, kissing me voraciously.

Fuck it. Fine.

I pin her against the shower wall and give her more than she bargained for.

She groans her approval.

She feels so good, oh God, she sure as hell does, so, so, so good, but this isn't what I had in mind. I pivot away from the wall, reach out behind her and turn off the water, still holding her entire body weight in my arms. She's attacking me, devouring me, fucking me, but I walk us into the bedroom as she continues slamming her body up and down on top of me. Holy shit, how I'm managing to even think right now, let alone walk, I have no idea.

I lay her down on the bed and pull out of her.

"No," she screams. "No, no, no! Get back in here!"

Oh God, I love it when she's bossy. When is she going to learn that I'm running this show? I head down between her legs to lick her sweet spot.

"No, no, no," she yells. Her eyes are wild. Her hair is soaking wet. Her olive skin is slick and wet and sexy as hell. "I'm in charge this time, Jonas—" But then my tongue finds her bull's-eye and she moans. "Oh, yeah," she breathes. "Just like that." She arches her back into me. "Oh, Jonas."

I don't know why she always fights me. When will she learn I know what's best for her?

I make love to her with my tongue and mouth, and she writhes against me.

"Jonas . . ." She sighs loudly. But she's still fighting me, battling to exert her will.

I keep working her, sliding my tongue around and around and over and across—employing every little trick that unlocks her. I've learned my baby oh so well by now.

"I want to lick you, Jonas," she says, gyrating. "I want to bring you to your knees." It always comes down to that, doesn't it? She wants to conquer me as much as I want to conquer her.

"No," I mumble, and keep going. I'm too turned on to stop what I'm doing. Oh, how I love breaking my little bucking bronco.

She squirms against me. "Yes," she moans. She lets out a sound I've heard from her before. It means she's getting close. And so am I. Oh yeah, I'm getting really turned on now. But she's still battling me. Why, I don't know. Doesn't she know resisting me is futile?

I keep at her, doing all the things she loves best. Oh God, I love the taste of her, the sounds she makes. There's no way I'm letting her take charge of me right now, no way I'm stopping what I'm doing, no fucking way.

She groans loudly. "I want to lick you, Jonas," she groans out again.

I ignore her. I don't know why her bossy bullshit always turns me on so much, but it does. I'm in a frenzy right now, reveling in her. Nothing can stop me now.

She moans again. "At the same time, baby," she breathes.

My eyes spring open. What?

"At the same time," she says again, shoving herself into me desperately.

Oh, well, that's something else entirely.

I look up at her from between her legs. She's lifts her head and smiles down at me, her eyelids at half-mast, her cheeks rosy. She's got that bad girl look in her eyes I love so much.

"At the same time," she repeats, trembling. She reaches down and grabs a fistful of my hair. "I want to lick you at the same time," she whispers, yanking roughly on my hair. "I've never done that. I wanna try it. Show me." She tugs at my hair again, really hard.

"Ow."

"Come on."

Here I thought I was going to make love to her, slowly, tenderly, whispering my devotion into her ear—and this angel of a woman wants to *sixty-nine* me? For the hundredth time since that first email from My Beautiful Intake Agent landed in my inbox, I'm in awe of her. She's not like anybody else.

I crawl over her, my chest heaving, my hard-on straining. She's spread-eagle underneath me. It's taking all my restraint not to plunge into her right now.

She licks her lips and nods. "At the same time," she says again, this time into my lips. "I wanna try it."

I nod vigorously and kiss her mouth.

She laps at my tongue. "Show me how." She guides me off her onto my back and grabs my shaft. She leans down like she's going to suck me.

"No, no, baby, not like that," I coo softly. My heart is racing. I'm so turned on I can barely contain myself.

She fondles me like she owns me. "How, then?" Her entire body has begun jerking and jolting, she's so aroused.

"You trust me?" My voice is hoarse.

"Mmm hmm." She continues touching me.

I remove her hands from me, gently. "I'm too close," I say. "You can't..."

She smiles. She likes pushing me over the edge as much I like pushing her. We're always at cross-purposes, she and I—too much alike, I suppose.

"You trust me?" I choke out again.

She nods.

"Say it."

"Yes." She shudders. "Yes, Jonas, completely. Come on."

"Lie this way." I point at the bed, indicating I want her to lie face up across the width of the bed.

She complies, writhing, trembling, ready to go off like a bottle rocket.

I pull her shoulders to the very edge of the bed, until her head is hanging off. And then I stand astride her face, one leg on either side of her head, gazing over the full length of her naked body.

I look straight down. Her face beams up at me from underneath my junk. I almost laugh out loud at the sight of her smiling underneath me. I can't believe she just asked to do this with me. And *now* of all times, when the entire world is falling down around us and any other woman would want me to hold her and comfort her and whisper sweet nothings in her ear.

"Baby, listen to me." I take a deep breath. "This turns me on—like, it drives me fucking crazy. So let me get going on you first for a bit, 'til you're just about to come, okay? Don't start in on me 'til you're almost there, like right on the edge, or else I'm never gonna make it. I can barely get through this, even without you sucking me off, it's just so fucking hot for me."

She nods and smiles.

"Promise?" I ask.

She nods. "Yep." But then she lifts her head and licks the entire length of me, from my balls all the way to my tip.

My knees buckle and I shudder.

"Okay, I'm ready now," she says.

I shake violently. "Don't do that again." She obviously doesn't understand how close I am and how much strength this is going to require.

She laughs again.

"Only when you're on the absolute edge," I repeat, my voice much firmer than it probably needs to be—but she needs to understand I absolutely cannot do this if she's going to tease me or start in on me too early. I'm going to need all my strength to do this, physical and otherwise. "Promise me." My voice is stern.

"Jeez," she says. "Okay, I promise, Lord-God-Master."

I exhale and reach down, and then I cradle my arms around her back and pull her entire torso up and up and up, 'til her belly is flush against my chest and her sweet pussy is right up against my mouth. She squeals and instinctively wraps her legs around my neck.

Oh God, I already feel like I'm going to lose it, just holding her in this position. I swallow hard. Her sweet spot is half an inch from my face. Her legs are a vise around my head. This woman is going to be the death of me, I swear to God. I lean in and lick her gently, with hardly any pressure at all. Just a taste.

She shrieks with glee. "This is so wild." She laughs.

But those are her last coherent words. In no time at all, I'm too turned on to be playful or gentle anymore. At this reverse angle—upside down—I can penetrate her, explore her, devour her like she's never experienced before. Within seconds, she's a hot mess, her body jerking against my face, her shrieks and screams and moans and howls a fucking symphony. And I'm losing my mind right along with her.

I convulse with my pleasure, my chest and arm muscles straining. Sweat pours down my back. It's taking every bit of my strength to keep holding her up like this, especially with her jerking around like a fish on a line. And I'm loving it. I don't need any more stimulation than this, don't need anything for myself, couldn't possibly handle anything more... Oh God, oh God, she flutters into my mouth, sending my skin jolting like she's zapped me with a Taser.

She lets out an epic roar and takes my full length into her warm, wet mouth, nice and deep... Oh my God, the way she's sucking on me is... And she tastes incredible... Fuck, oh fuck, she's so fucking talented, even upside down.

If there's a heaven, I think we just found it.

My knees buckle but I readjust.

Holy shit.

Oh God, she's really good at this. So, so good. And she tastes so fucking good.

She's making crazy-ass sounds, and so am I.

This is incredible. I can't . . .

Thank you, God, for letting me experience this kind of ecstasy at least once before I die.

Her tongue does something particularly insightful, and my entire body jerks. I'm not sure if this is pleasure or pain. A swirl of light flashes behind my eyelids. My knees buckle. The sound emerging from me is the sound of a lunatic, but I can't stop. I'm hanging on by the barest of threads. My muscles strain to hold her up. Her mouth is voracious, and so is mine.

Her entire body jerks violently and she lets loose with a pained howl. Her body slams open and shut against my tongue like a window left unlatched in a storm.

I yank myself out of her mouth feverishly, my knees buckling again.

She shrieks.

I want nothing more than to remain inside her warm mouth and see this thing through to its natural, mutual conclusion, but pulling out is an involuntary act, an instinctive act of self-preservation. She's still brand new to climaxing, just a newborn colt, and I'm betting my dick she's gonna clench her jaw like a motherfucker when she comes. I love her, God knows I do, and I'm willing to let her do just about anything to me—*except* reflexively chomp down on my cock like a great white shark on a sea lion.

I throw her down on the bed, quickly pounce between her legs, and slam myself into her, letting her orgasm undulate around me. When my release comes, I'm pretty sure I lose consciousness for a split second. My chest heaves. Sweat pours down my back. I can't breathe. I can't think. I can't... I can't ... I can't do a fucking thing but lie motionless on top of her and catch my breath. I'm not thinking anything coherent right now—other than maybe, "holy fuck."

After a minute, I roll onto my back next to her, shaking and gasping for air. I'm soaking wet. Damn, that was a work out. Fuck. My entire body burns with the exertion of what we just did.

She rolls onto her side and props her head up on her elbow. Her cheeks are flushed. "So that's sixty-nining, huh?" She laughs. "I thought it was... simpler. How the hell does anyone besides a Greek god like you ever accomplish that?"

I swallow hard, still not completely functional. "That was the super-advanced way to do it," I manage to say. "There are several other ways." I breathe deeply. I'm still shaking. That took a lot out of me, in every way. "Much, much easier ways."

She laughs again. "Well, damn, boy, let's try every which way." She grins broadly. "We'll just go right on down the list."

I laugh. She can always make me laugh like no one else can. "I'm in favor of that strategy."

She hoots. "Oh, Jonas. How the hell were you able to hold me up like that? Holy moly." She squeezes my bicep. "You truly are *man-ness,* Jonas Faraday. My manly man-ness-y manly man."

I laugh again. "I could only do it because you're so damned limber and strong. You're the reason that worked."

She beams at me. We've discovered yet another way we're a match made in heaven. I suddenly have an actual, coherent thought: *I love this woman more than I ever thought possible.*

My heart continues racing. "I thought I was going to pass out for a minute there," I say. "I was seeing stars."

"Oh God." She laughs. "That wouldn't have been good with me in that position."

I sit up and touch her face. I'm suddenly earnest. "I'd never let anything happen to you. You know that, right?"

Her entire face contorts like I just gave her a puppy.

I love this woman. I want to tell her so. I want to look into her eyes and say those three little words. I want her to understand they're not just words to me—that they're my new religion. I want her to know I've never said those words to anyone else, that I've been reserving them, waiting my whole life to say them to *her*.

But nothing comes out of my mouth. Again. What's wrong with me?

She beams at me. "I know that," she says softly. "I trust you. That's why this works."

I know the "this" she's referring to isn't the elusive "cascading sixty-nine." No, the "this" she means is "Jonas and Sarah"—the two of us, together. It's our off-the-charts chemistry. It's how she gets me and I get her. It's how she makes me laugh when no one else can. It's how I told her about what happened to my mother—even the parts I'm ashamed of, even the parts that reveal my worthlessness—and she didn't run away. It's how I cried to her, sobbed to her, actually— even though I'd sworn off crying a long time ago. And it's especially how she held me close and cried along with me.

I look over at her. She beams at me.

On second thought, maybe the "this" she's referring to isn't "Jonas and Sarah," after all. Maybe the "this" is just Sarah herself, the new Sarah who's learning to let go and claim her deepest desires. Because now that she's given free rein to what she wants rather than what she's supposed to want, she's becoming a new woman every single day, right before my eyes. I can see it, plain as day. Fuck, anyone could see it. It's in the way she walks, the way she talks. The way she struts. The way she fucks. Maybe I'm just along for the ride, her instrument of self-discovery, a mere conduit to her most powerful self. I don't know. And I don't care. As long as I get to be the one lying next to her, the one making love to her, the one fucking her brains out if that's what she wants, whatever, I don't give a fuck what the "this" is she's referring to. As long as it includes me, I'm in.

I rub my hands over my face. Jesus, this woman is my crack.

There's a beat. I should say it now. But I want to say it when I can show her and tell her at the same time. I don't trust myself with words alone—they've been a struggle for me ever since that whole year as a kid when I didn't speak at all.

She clears her throat. "How is it possible every single time gets better and better and better?" she asks.

"Because we were made for each other," I say softly. *And because I love you.*

Her smile widens. She pushes me back onto the bed and swiftly straddles my lap. She leans down and kisses me tenderly.

I rest my hands on her thighs. "Where the hell did you get the idea to sixty-nine me all of a sudden?" I ask. "That was a pleasant surprise."

She looks at me sideways. "Jonas, I've been reading sex club applications for the past three months, remember? I've been stockpiling ideas the whole time." She winks.

"Oh yeah?" I like where this is headed. "You've picked up an idea or two, have you?" I cross my arms under my head and gaze up at her.

"Yes, sir," she says, her eyes ablaze. She rubs her hands along my biceps. "Maybe just a thing or two... and now that I've got the right partner... the perfect partner..." She leans down again and kisses me. "My sweet Jonas."

My heart leaps. "Sarah," I breathe. I want to tell her. She deserves to hear it from me.

She whispers right into my ear. "Madness."

I exhale and close my eyes.

I know I should be happy to hear this word—she's telling me she loves me in the exact way I've taught her to say it to me—the precise way I've trained her to say it so as not to scare me off. *Love is a serious mental disease,* I explained to her, over and over, quoting Plato—pointedly avoiding the more pedantic but direct route to the same message. I glance away, trying to collect my thoughts. I feel like I'm failing her with all my secret codes.

"Oh, Jonas." She leans down and peppers my entire face with soft kisses—the thing she does that makes me want to crawl into her arms and cry like a baby. "Don't think so much. Thinking is the enemy."

"That's *my* line," I say.

She nods. "Then you have no excuse." She runs her fingers over the tattoo on my left forearm, sending a shiver up my spine. *For a man to conquer himself is the first and noblest of all victories.*

I close my eyes. She's right. I inhale deeply.

She caresses my right forearm with her other hand. *Visualize the divine originals.* And then she runs her fingers from my tattoos to my biceps, to my shoulders, and across my bare chest, tracing every crease and indentation and ripple along the way.

She's right. I need to stop thinking so much. *Love is a serious mental disease.* Yes. *Madness.* Why am I freaking out about the exact words we use? The feelings are there, I know they are—for both of us. The words don't matter.

Her fingers migrate downward to the ruts and ridges of my abs.

I exhale. She knows how I feel. With every touch, with every kiss, she's telling me she does, and that she feels the same way. Why am I over-thinking this?

"Hey, remember my 'sexual preferences' section on my application?" she asks.

She means her so-called verbal application to the Jonas Faraday Club—the application she refused to write out for me in detail because she's a royal pain in the ass.

"As I recall, you summarized the entirety of your 'sexual preferences' with two little words."

Her fingers move to my belly button. "Jonas Faraday," she says, poking me with her finger. She slides her fingers from my belly all the way up to my mouth and begins lightly tracing my lips. I kiss the tip of her finger and she smiles. I grab her hand and pretend to eat the sexy ring on her thumb like I'm the Cookie Monster. Her smile gives way to a giggle. She sticks her thumb in my mouth and I suck on it. She laughs with glee.

"And that's still one hundred percent accurate," she says, pulling her thumb out of my mouth. "*Jonas Faraday.* Mmm hmm." She leans down and skims her lips against mine. "But I think I've got a few... um... *additions* to my 'sexual preferences' section—ideas I've been stockpiling over the past three months. We'll call it an *addendum* to my application." She laughs again and kisses me full on the mouth.

I feel like I'm holding a lottery ticket and she's about to announce I've got the winning numbers. "What kinds of ideas?"

She smiles wickedly. She knows I'm on pins and needles and she's enjoying torturing me. "Well, I'm still formulating the exact specifications of my addendum," she says coyly. "And you're only on a need-to-know basis, anyway."

I frown.

"But I promise you one thing, my sweet Jonas—whatever I come up with, it's gonna bring you to your frickin' knees."

Chapter 3

Sarah

At Josh's arrival, Jonas is a new man. Other than when Jonas and I were going at it like upside-down-intertwined-X-rated-*Cirque-du-Soleil* performers a couple hours ago—and let me just say an enthusiastic *woot woot* and a hearty *hellz yeah* in fond memory of that acrobatic deliciousness—this is by far the most comfortable and confident I've seen Jonas since we discovered my ransacked apartment earlier today.

"Hey," Josh says, putting down his duffel bag and bro-hugging Jonas. "Well, hello, Sarah Cruz." He embraces me next. "Fancy meeting you here."

"Get used to it," Jonas says. He winks at me and I smile back. Jonas has made it abundantly clear he's elated I'm here, regardless of the circumstances.

"So what the hell's going on?" Josh asks, concern unfurling across his face.

In all the chaos of our return from Belize, Jonas hasn't yet told Josh what's happened. And, damn, there's a lot to tell him—not the least of which is how Jonas applied to this depraved thing called The Club, and, oh yeah, how Sarah worked for said depraved club, and oh yeah, how we've recently discovered it's just a global brothel, and, hey, guess what, the bastards just ransacked Sarah's and Kat's apartments and stole their computers. All Jonas said over the phone to Josh was "I need you" and Josh hopped a plane, no questions asked. But now it's time for details.

Jonas moans. "It's so fucked up, man."

Josh sits down on the couch, his face etched with anxiety. "Tell me."

Jonas sits down next to him, sighing like he doesn't know where to begin. He runs his hand through his hair and exhales loudly.

I don't blame Jonas for feeling overwhelmed—he's got a helluva lot of ground to cover. But before Jonas begins speaking, Kat comes out of the bathroom and strides into the room like she owns the place. Josh glances toward her movement, and then away, and then does a double take worthy of Bugs Bunny. The man might as well be shouting "bawoooooooga!" at the sight of her while his eyeballs telescope in and out of his head.

I would have thought Mr. Parties-with-Justin-Timberlake would have a bit more game than a cartoon rabbit—but, no, apparently not. Silly me, I should have known no mortal man, whether he has celebrity friends or not, can play it cool upon first beholding the golden loveliness of Katherine "Kat" Morgan. The woman is every teenage-boy's fantasy sprung to life—the tomboy-girl-next-door who goes off to college and comes back home a gorgeous and curvy and vivacious movie star (except, of course, that Kat works in PR). Why would Josh, unlike so many before him, be immune to Kat's special blend of charm, beauty and charisma?

Kat sashays right up to Josh like he flew to Seattle just to see her.

"I'm Kat—Sarah's best friend." She puts out her hand.

Josh smiles broadly. "Josh." He shakes her hand with mock politeness. "Jonas' brother." I can feel the electricity between them from ten feet away.

"I know," she says. "I read the article." She motions to the business magazine on the coffee table, the one with Jonas and Josh on the cover wearing their tailored suits. "I sure hope you're more complicated than that article makes you out to be."

Josh looks at Jonas for an explanation, but Jonas shrugs.

"If the article is to be believed," Kat explains, "Jonas is the 'enigmatic loner-investment-wunderkind' twin—and you're just the simple *playboy*."

Josh laughs. "That's what the article said?"

"In so many words."

"Hmm." He smirks. "Interesting. And if someone were writing a magazine article about you, what gross over-simplification would they use?"

Kat thinks for a minute. "I'd be 'a party girl with a heart of gold.'" She shoots me a snarky look—that's the phrase I always use to describe her.

Josh smiles broadly. "How come I only get a one-word description—playboy—and you get a whole phrase?"

Kat shrugs. "Okay, party girl, then."

"That's two words."

She raises an eyebrow. "In this hypothetical magazine article about me, they'd spell it with a hyphen."

Oh, man. *Ka-pow.* Talk about instant chemistry. I look at Jonas and I can tell he's thinking exactly what I am—*get a room*—albeit in some warped Jonas Faraday kind of way, I'm sure.

"So what's going on here, Party Girl with a Hyphen?" Josh asks. "I take it we didn't all congregate here to party?"

"No, unfortunately," Kat says. "Though, hey, we did have some of your tequila earlier, so thanks for that." She twists her mouth. "No, I'm just here to support Sarah—and, well, I think I might be some kind of refugee in all this, too." She looks at me sympathetically. "Although I think maybe Jonas is being slightly overprotective having me stay here. I'm not sure yet."

Jonas bristles and clenches his jaw, obviously not thrilled at being called overprotective.

"You're a refugee in all this?" Josh asks. He looks at Jonas, confounded. "What the fuck's going on, Jonas?"

Jonas grunts, yet again. "Sit down."

Josh and Jonas sit.

Jonas takes a deep breath and starts to explain, beginning with Stacy's yellow-bracelet-clad appearance and diatribe at the sports bar, then moving on to our "amazing" trip to Belize and the scary surprise we discovered in my apartment upon our return, and finishing up with his extreme concern that The Club might try to ensure my silence through means more violent than stealing my computer and wrecking my apartment. Throughout it all, Josh listens intently—nodding, pursing his lips, and occasionally glancing at Kat and me. For our part, Kat and I don't make a peep while Jonas speaks, though we exchange a crap-ton of meaningful glances, smirks, and raised eyebrows the entire time.

In addition to engaging in a near-constant nonverbal dialogue with Kat, I also make several observations while Jonas speaks. One—and I realize this is totally irrelevant to the situation at large—holy frickin' moly, Jonas Faraday turns me on, oh yeah, boy howdy, booyah, hellz yeah, whoa doggie, there's no doubt about it. Just watching his luscious lips move when he speaks—and how he licks them when he's pausing to think—and how one side of his mouth rides up a little bit when he's making a wry observation—just seeing the intelligence and intensity in his eyes and noticing the tattoos on his forearms and the bulge of his biceps when he runs his hands through his hair—and a thousand other things about him, too, all of them heart-palpitation-inducing—it's enough to make me want to get all over that boy like tie dye on a hippie.

Gah.

The second observation that leaps out at me while Jonas is speaking is that, man oh man, my supernaturally good-lookin' boyfriend's got the hots for me, too—like, *oh my God,* so, so bad—and, looping back to observation number one, that effing turns me on like boom on a bomb. Perhaps I shouldn't be so turned on by *him* being so turned on by *me,* considering the circumstances—I'm certain I should be consumed with fear and apprehension instead of my hormones right now—but I can't help myself. When Jonas says Belize was "life-changing" for him and calls me "magnificent" and "smart as hell" and "wise," and when he stutters a bit and blushes like a vine-ripened tomato when he says all of it, I feel like he's standing on a mountaintop declaring his raging, thumping, ardent desire for me. *And it turns me on.*

I've never felt so adored and safe and free to be me in my whole life as I am with Jonas. It's like I'm a big ol' vat of mustard—just yellow mustard and nothing else—and up 'til now I've lived my whole life worrying the guys I'm attracted to, the guys who *say* they really, really like mustard, might actually crave a little ketchup or relish or mayo to go along with their mustard, at least occasionally—and who could blame them? And then, all of a sudden, through dumb luck in the most unexpected way, I've stumbled upon the hottest guy in the universe *who happens to have a bizarre mustard fetish,* an insatiable appetite for frickin' mustard to the exclusion of all other condiments! It's like I can't lose, no matter what I say or do or think *because I'm goddamned mustard, bitches.* It's blowing my mind and wreaking havoc on my body to be adored like this, to be *seen* and *understood* and *accepted* so completely. Not to mention fucked so brilliantly. Jonas fucked me so well in Belize, a howler monkey outside our tree house lit a cigarette.

It's like I've been bottled up my whole life and this beautiful man has *uncorked* me. Yes, that's it—I'm frickin' *uncorked*, baby. *Pop!* And now that I am, all I keep thinking about is giving my sweet Jonas, my Hottie McHottie of a boyfriend—my baby, my love, my manly man with sad eyes and luscious lips—pleasure and excitement and thrills and chills and orgasms and assurances and safety and adoration and understanding and acceptance and good old fashioned fuckery like nothing *he's* experienced before—"untethering" *him* the way he's so profoundly untethered *me*.

Gah.

But enough about that. For now. Obviously, we've got bigger fish to fry than satisfying my insatiable lady-boner for the supremely gorgeous Jonas Faraday.

Focus, focus, focus.

Whew.

The third (and more germane) observation I make while my muscled, rippling, smokin' hot, hunky-monkey of a boyfriend speaks to his brother—wooh! I just made myself hot for him again—is that Jonas noticeably doesn't start his explanation to Josh by mentioning any details about The Club—neither its existence nor its purported premise. At first, I'm confused by that omission, but quickly it becomes clear that particular piece of exposition isn't at all necessary... because... wait for it... *Josh already knows all about The Club*. And even more surprising than that, it's also quite clear, based on a couple things Jonas says—for example, "Hey, Josh, did you keep any of your emails from them?"—that Josh himself was a member of The Club at some point before Jonas.

The minute that shocking but fascinating cat lurches out of its bag, Kat shoots me a look that says "holy shitballs"—and I acknowledge her expression with a "holy crappola" look of my own. Very, very interesting. Apparently, neither Faraday apple fell too far from the Faraday horndog tree.

But although I'm surprised to find out about Josh's membership, I'm not fazed by it. Maybe it's because I've processed so many applications, including relatively tame ones from globetrotters like Josh, most of them perfectly normal and sweet. Or maybe it's because, since meeting Jonas, my own rampant sex drive has enslaved me and turned me into a horndog, too—so how could I presume to judge anyone else?

Or maybe, just maybe, I'm so damned grateful Jonas applied to The Club (or else how would we have met?), thrilled by the masterful way he touches me and makes love to me like no one ever has, spellbound by his unquenchable quest to satisfy me, enraptured by his determination to do all things "excellently" that I'm now inclined to view heightened or avid sexual desire as a magnificent superpower rather than something to disparage or snub. Whatever the reason, whatever the journey, whatever the delusion, the bottom line is I'm feeling pretty nonjudgmental about Josh being a past member of The Club right about now.

But that doesn't mean I'm not hella *curious* about it. Because I am.

I don't mean I'm *curious* in some kind of winky-winky code, like "Hello, I'm a freak show who's *curious* (wink, wink) about her boyfriend's brother." Ew. No. Not at all. What I mean is I'm *intellectually* curious to know the details about Josh's (or *anyone's*) successful club experience. After three months of reviewing applications on the front-end of the intake process, I still have no idea what happens on the back-end of it—that is, *after* a member receives his welcome package. And I admit, I really, really want to know.

What did The Club deliver to Josh during his membership period? Who were the women and what were they like? Did he see any of them repeatedly? Did he form emotional attachments to any of them? What the heck did they do to him/with him/for him that he felt he couldn't get outside the clandestine walls of The Club? Did he ever suspect what was really going on—that these women were hired to say and do and be whatever he'd requested in his application—or did he buy the entire fantasy, hook-line-and-sinker? And if he *did* suspect the truth about these women, did he care?

And, of course, the granddaddy question of them all, the thing I'm dying to know more than anything else (though I'm not proud to admit it): What did Josh request in his frickin' application in the first place? Color me curious, I gotta know.

31

My educated guess is that, given Josh's good looks and penchant for exploring the world, he's one of those world traveler/tycoon/professional-athlete types who joined The Club as a simple and expeditious means of finding good sex and compatible companionship wherever he happened to roam—as opposed to being a wack job looking for *bukkake* or for someone to poop on his face. But, hey, maybe Josh isn't what he appears to be. Perhaps there's something more wack jobby about him than initially meets the eye. I can't help but wonder. And judging by the look on Kat's face, she can't help but wonder, either—oh my goodness, yes, it's quite clear to me little miss Kitty Kat's wondering herself into a frenzy right now.

I'm not surprised by that zealous twinkle in Kat's eye, to be honest. From the moment Kat found out about my intake agent job, she's tried relentlessly (though unsuccessfully) to pry every juicy detail out of me about every application I've processed. And it wasn't my intake agent job that ignited Kat's sexual curiosity—she's always been this way.

As long as I've known her, Kat's been the boy-crazy one of the two of us, sexually supercharged from an early age, for some reason not shackled by the usual hang-ups and inhibitions that seem to plague other girls, including me. Before Jonas came into my life, I used to watch Kat glide through her interactions with members of the opposite sex and marvel about her supernatural confidence and almost masculine libido. But now that Jonas has "unlocked" me, I have a totally different perspective. In fact, my post-Jonas self might even give Kitty Kat a run for her sexually supercharged money.

I glance at Kat—and when I see her flushed and tantalized face, I suddenly worry my facial expression matches hers. If that's the case, if I look half as revved up as she does right now, then I'm going to hell in a handbasket. Intellectual curiosity or not, no matter how innocent or anthropological in nature my wonderings might be, I absolutely can't be thinking about my boyfriend's brother's sex life. Period. I can't indulge my sexual curiosity, intellectual or otherwise, with or about anyone besides my sweet Jonas—and least of all not regarding his twin brother. I just have to let it go. Some things are not meant to be known by me. Boom. Truth. But that doesn't mean Kat has to let it go, not at all. And by the look on her face, she doesn't plan to.

The next thing I observe during Jonas' telling of his saga occurs to me precisely when he gets to the "and then it turned out Stacy was a fucking prostitute" part of his story. Whereas Jonas quite obviously feels acute humiliation and even suppressed rage all over again simply by *talking* about the fiasco, Josh on the other hand seems oddly calm about the whole thing. Amused, even. He's certainly in no danger of escaping into the bathroom to process his emotions or punch a hole in the wall, that's for sure.

"Huh," Josh finally says when Jonas finishes talking. "Interesting."

Jonas exhales with impatience. His jaw muscles pulse. Clearly, he was expecting something else from Josh.

"Wow," Josh adds, shaking his head. He considers something for a moment. "I'm not sure, bro. I met some really great girls."

Kat visibly scowls.

I can't resist asking at least one, teeny-tiny question. "How long was your membership, Josh?"

"A month."

I'm relieved. That means he's probably not a total wack job. I steal a glance at Jonas. Oh man, he's fuming. At me for asking the question? At himself for joining for a year? Or at Josh's milk-toast reaction to the whole situation? I'm not sure about the source of Jonas' ire—but I figure it couldn't hurt for me to ask one more teensy-weensy question.

"And you... completed your entire membership period... successfully?"

"Oh, yeah. Definitely." Josh smiles broadly. He thinks for a minute. "There's no way all those girls were prostitutes. They were super cool, all of them."

All those girls? All of them? How many women are we talking about here?

"They were *all* super cool, huh?" I say, even though I know I should shut the hell up. "Well, Julia Roberts was 'super cool' in *Pretty Woman*, too."

Josh laughs. "True."

Jonas' eyes flash. What's going on in that beautiful head of his? He looks like he's on the verge of exploding.

"How many women could you possibly have gone through in a

month?" Kat asks, swooping in to ask the precise thing I'm wondering myself.

Josh's eyes latch onto Kat with laser sharpness.

"I mean . . ." Kat's face turns red. But she can't figure out how to make her question sound pertinent to anything other than her own salacious and highly personal desire to know.

Josh stares at Kat without apology for a very long beat. "A couple," he finally answers slowly. But he's not even trying to sound like he's telling her the truth. He flashes her a broad smile.

Oh boy, he's definitely a Faraday. No doubt about it.

Bam. Just like that, I have a sudden, disgusting thought.

"Josh, did you ever use your membership to meet a 'super cool' girl in the Seattle area?"

Josh's smile droops with instant understanding. He nods slowly. "Once."

Oh no. Please tell me Josh and Jonas didn't both have sex with Stacy the Faker. My stomach churns at the thought.

Jonas' mortified face tells me he gets my meaning, too. "Brunette. Piercing blue eyes—like the bluest eyes you've ever seen—fair skin." It's like he's rattling off a grocery list. "C-cup. Perfect teeth. Smokin' hot body—" He looks at me apologetically. "Sorry, baby."

But there's no need to apologize. Stacy *does* have a smokin' hot body. And, frankly, I like that she does—the hotter the better. My hunkalicious man wanted *me*, sight unseen, based solely on my brains and personality, and he fantasized about me while screwing another woman—a woman with a smokin' hot body. I've got no problem with that. In fact, the thought gets me going like a hungry dog on a ragged bone.

"It's okay." I wink at Jonas. *Woof.*

One side of his mouth curls up, and for one fleeting, delicious moment, I know we're both thinking about our first phone conversation, the one that unexpectedly devolved into dirty phone sex.

Josh is visibly relieved. "No," he says, exhaling "That doesn't describe my Seattle girl. When I filled out my application, I requested only—" He stops mid-sentence. He looks at Kat and smashes his mouth into a hard line.

What? Oh my God. *What?* I've got to know! He requested only... what? Black women? Plus sized beauties? Asian women? A-cups? Men? *Transgenders?* I'm horrible, I admit it, depraved, perverted, going to hell, but I'm dying to know what was on the tip of Josh's tongue. Damn!

But Josh obviously isn't going to elaborate. "Thank God, bro," Josh says. "That would have been just like having sex with *you."* He mock-shudders, obviously highly amused.

Jonas isn't amused at all. "We're totally off track here," he says, exasperated. "The only thing that matters is that these bastards have fucked with Sarah and Kat, and we have no way of knowing whether they're done fucking with them or if they're just getting started."

Josh leans back on the couch. He sighs audibly. "I don't know."

Jonas lets out a loud puff of air. "What the fuck does that mean?" He stands. His jaw muscles are pulsing. "What the fuck don't you *know?"*

There's a beat as Josh tries to process Jonas' sudden flash of anger.

"You don't fucking know *what?"* Jonas booms. Oh man, he's gone from zero to sixty in a heartbeat.

"Hey, man, calm down. Just... Jesus, Jonas. Sit down."

Jonas' entire body tenses. Every muscle bulges. "Fuck that! Fuck everything except 'What do you need from me, Jonas?' Fuck everything except 'I'm with you, man, one hundred and ten percent!' I'm not gonna sit around and wait to find out if these fuckers have something more planned for us. I'm taking them down."

"Sit down, Jonas," Josh says emphatically. "Let's just talk about this for a minute, rationally."

"Oh, *you're* gonna tell *me* how to be rational? Mr. Buys-a-Lamborghini-on-a-Fucking-Whim-When-His-Girlfriend-Breaks-Up-With-Him is gonna tell *me* to be rational?"

Josh rolls his eyes. "I'm just saying I don't know, that's all. I'm not saying 'I disagree.' Big difference. Just sit the fuck down for a minute. Jesus, Jonas."

"What the fuck don't you *know?* There's nothing to decide. I'm telling you they've fucked with my girl. That's all you need to know! End of story." He's started prancing around the room like a boxer about to get into the ring.

"Jonas!" Josh yells.

Jonas' eyes are blazing.

"Sit the fuck down. Come on."

Jonas grabs his hair in frustration.

"Please."

Jonas grumbles loudly, but he complies. His eyes are on fire. And so is the rest of him. Holy Baby Jesus in a wicker basket, he's so frickin' hot right now, I want to tie him up and make him beg me for mercy.

"Thank you," Josh says politely. He exhales pointedly. "You get so riled up sometimes, man." He shakes his head.

Jonas is trembling. And so am I, just watching him. Oh man, he's a beast—a sexy frickin' beast.

"Okay. Now take a deep breath for a second."

Jonas glares at him.

"Do it."

After a minute, Jonas begrudgingly makes a big show of breathing deeply, as requested, but it's hard to tell if the exercise is calming him down or pissing him off.

"Good. *Good.* Thank you. I'm on your team, bro—I'm *always* on your team. No questions asked, no matter what. Always. One hundred ten percent."

Jonas nods. He knows that. Of course, he does. Without a doubt.

I glance at Kat. She's sitting on the edge of her seat in the corner, her eyes wide.

"Just take a second, man," Josh continues. "Don't fly off the handle. We'll just talk about it, man to man, okay? Talking it through doesn't mean we're having a disagreement—we're just talking it through to consider all angles." Josh keeps his voice calm. Something tells me he's talked Jonas off the ledge a time or two—and maybe even literally for all I know. There's still so much I don't know about Jonas and his demons.

"Don't talk to me like I'm eight years old," Jonas huffs. "I've read that stupid book, too, you know. 'Talking about it doesn't mean we're disagreeing.' Find a new bullshit line, man. That one's stale."

Josh laughs. "It's all I've got—the only thing I remember from that stupid book. Don't take away my one smart thing to say. Not everybody's got a photographic memory like you, motherfucker."

Jonas nods and exhales, regaining control of himself.

Interesting.

"Let's just talk it through," Josh continues. He smirks. "*Talking* about it doesn't mean we're *disagreeing*."

Jonas rolls his eyes. "So I've heard. Repeatedly."

Josh flashes a wide smile.

It seems they've reached some kind of common ground.

Kat and I exchange a "what the hell just happened?" glance. Neither of us speaks.

Josh breathes deeply, in through his nose and out through his mouth, obviously trying to lure Jonas into following suit—and Jonas does. It's like Josh is some kind of gorilla-whisperer or something. And it's working—I can see Jonas calming down with each breath. It's fascinating to watch. And a total turn-on, too.

"Okay. Let's think," Josh says. "What's the point in taking down the entire organization? I mean, really? Just *think* about it, logically. That sounds like an awfully big job—and maybe overkill. Think about it, Jonas. Yes, we've got to protect Sarah and Kat, of course . . ." He smiles at me and then at Kat. "*Of course.* And we will. I promise. But beyond that, why do we care what The Club does?"

I note Josh's adoption of "we" rather than "you" in that last sentence. Very well done.

Jonas shifts in his seat. He's considering.

"Why kill a fly with a sledgehammer when a flyswatter will do?"

A muscle in Jonas' jaw pulses.

Josh barrels ahead. "The Club provides a service—and very well, I might add, speaking from experience. So, yeah, maybe things aren't exactly as they appear, maybe they oversell the fantasy a bit—but so does Disneyland. I mean, you can go ride a rollercoaster anywhere, right?—but you pay ten times more to ride that same roller coaster at Disneyland. Why? Because it's got Mickey Mouse's face on it." Josh nods, thoroughly convinced by his own logic.

Jonas huffs but doesn't speak. His eyes are like granite.

"Maybe all these guys who join The Club want to ride a roller coaster with Mickey Mouse's face on it—and they're happy as clams to pay a shitload to do it. They don't even *want* to know they could ride the same roller coaster without Mickey's face on it for two bucks down the street."

Jonas bursts out of his skin. "Jesus, Josh," he says, jumping back up. "Really?" He's barely suppressing his fury. "'Live and let live?' Is that it? Let these guys go on their merry way while I sit around and wonder night and day if they're gonna come after my baby or not?" He's roaring now, absolutely enraged. "No fucking way."

I stand and put my hand on Jonas' forearm, signaling him to let me speak. He jerks his arm away, fuming. "I expected *you* of all people to understand," he seethes at Josh. "Fuck!"

I take a step back. He obviously doesn't want me to meddle. And he's right. I shouldn't have butted into this brother-to-brother conversation. Not yet. Not now.

"I *do* understand. I'm just saying let's narrow down exactly what we're trying to accomplish here."

There's a long beat.

Jonas is incapable of coherent speech. He's absolutely furious. After a long beat, he motions to me as if he's giving me the floor.

"Josh," I say. I feel the need to choose my words carefully. "Your premise is faulty. When you buy a ticket for Disneyland, you *know* you're signing up to ride a Mickey Mouse roller coaster. Not everyone signs up to ride a Mickey Mouse rollercoaster when they join The Club—but that's what they give them, anyway."

Josh looks genuinely confused.

I feel too stupid to say anything else. I sit back down on the couch, wishing I were invisible.

"What do you mean?" Josh asks me. He sounds remarkably sincere. The tone of his voice makes me look up at him. The expression on his face matches his voice.

Jonas exhales. "She means not everyone is totally fucked-up like you and me." He clears his throat. "Or, at least, like me—you seem to have been cured of your fuckeduppedness by that stupid book."

Josh can't help but laugh at that.

"She means some people are, you know, *normal*," Jonas continues. He sits down on the couch next to me and puts his arm around me. I guess that's his way of apologizing for jerking away a moment ago. If so, I accept his apology.

"What the fuck does that even mean?" Josh finally says. "*Normal?*"

Jonas doesn't answer.

"Okay, fine, let's say there are *normal* people out there. Why the fuck would any *normal* person join The Club?" He seems genuinely confounded.

"To find love," Jonas says quietly. "That's what normal people want. That's what The Club promises to the normal ones. And it's a scam."

Hearing Jonas adopt exactly what I've said to him, whether he believes it or not (I'm not completely sure he does) makes me tingle all over. He's telling me he's got my back along with the rest of my body parts.

Josh laughs derisively.

"It's true," I say, defending Jonas. Defending myself. Defending love, faith, hope, optimism—I don't know what the hell I'm defending. Maybe I'm still hung up on seeing my little software engineer's elated face when Stacy lied and said she only watched college basketball, just like him. Maybe I need to believe that love, and not just sex, is what truly what makes the world go around. Maybe I need to believe there's someone for everyone, no matter how fucked up or depraved. Maybe I just need to believe there are men out there who are absolutely nothing like my father.

Jonas grabs my hand and squeezes it. And with that simple gesture, he's telling me it's Jonas and me against the whole world. Screw anyone else who doesn't believe in true love. We know it's real.

Josh looks incredulous. "Seriously?" There's a beat as he studies Jonas. "Did *you* join The Club looking for love?'"

Jonas blanches. He looks at me, not sure how to respond. But Jonas doesn't need my permission to tell the truth. I know exactly why he joined The Club. And I don't care.

I nod, encouraging him.

Jonas brings the back of my hand to his lips and lays a soft kiss on my skin, his eyes burning with intensity. "No, I didn't."

"Well, neither did I. I can't imagine anyone ever would. That's pretty far-fetched—even if someone's *normal*." He winces at me. "Sorry, Sarah."

I nod. It's okay.

"I'm pretty sure I joined The Club because I was having some kind of mental breakdown," Jonas says softly, almost inaudibly. "Again."

Josh looks absolutely shocked.

"Though I didn't realize it at the time, of course." He looks at me pointedly. "I joined The Club because I didn't understand what was really going on with me, what I really wanted—or what I needed." He squeezes my hand. "I was spiraling, man."

My heart is thumping out of my chest.

Jonas' eyes are boring holes into mine. He's giving me that "I'm going to swallow you whole" look—and, holy hell, I want him to swallow me whole.

Josh clearly doesn't know what the hell to say.

The silence is deafening.

"Well, all righty, then," Kat finally says.

Josh exhales. "Holy shit, Jonas." He rubs his hands over his face, clearly at a loss as to how to handle his ever-complicated brother. "I'm all in when it comes to protecting Sarah and Kat, okay? Whatever it takes—you know that, right?"

"I know." Jonas exhales. "Thanks."

"I just think maybe you're overreacting about—"

"Fuck, Josh!" Jonas leaps to a stand and glowers over Josh on the couch. "These motherfuckers threatened my girl and her best friend. Do you understand? They crossed the fucking line!"

Josh stands and opens his mouth to speak, but Jonas cuts him off.

"I'm not letting them near her."

He pulls me up off the couch and into him like he's defending me from Josh—which is, I must say, a certifiably crazy thing to imply.

"I'm gonna protect her—which means decimating the fuck out of them. Do you understand me? *Decimating them.*" He's shaking. His muscles are bulging around me.

"Whoa," Josh says. "Calm down."

"I'm not gonna let it happen again, Josh. I couldn't survive it this time—I know I couldn't. I barely survived it before. You didn't see what I saw—the blood. It was everywhere. You weren't there." He shuts his eyes tight. "You didn't see her." He's flipping out. Oh my God, he's totally flipping out. "I'm not gonna let it happen again. I can't do it again."

His grip on me is stifling, but I wouldn't dream of pushing away, not right now.

40

Kat's mouth hangs open. I haven't had a chance to tell her anything about Belize—or about Jonas' tragic childhood.

Josh looks anguished. "Jonas... Oh my God."

"I thought *you'd* understand, of all people." Jonas's voice is thick with emotion. "I don't want to do this alone, but I will. I'll do whatever I have to do, don't you understand?" He squeezes me even tighter. "I can't let anything happen to her. Not again. Never again."

Oh my God, I'm turned on. Totally, thoroughly, completely turned on.

Poor Josh's face is stricken. "Ladies, could you give us a minute?" he says. He's at a total loss here. "Please."

Jonas juts his chin and squeezes me even tighter.

"Jonas," I whisper, my lips brushing softly against his jawline. "Talk to your brother, baby. He's on your team." My lips find his neck. His skin is hot. He's shaking. His grip on me is like a vise.

I'm not completely sure what's going on inside Jonas' head, but I'm damn near positive Josh is the one who can help him get his mind right again.

I reach up and touch his chiseled face. "Your brother's on your side," I say quietly. I brush my lips against his neck. He presses himself into me and I feel his erection against me. "Just listen to him," I continue. "He dropped everything to come here for you. Listen to him."

Jonas lets go of my hand, grabs my face with both hands, and kisses me like he owns me. Clearly, his kiss is meant to explain something to Josh, and not necessarily to me, but I'm not complaining. Yowza. He can use my lips to make a point to Josh any frickin' time he likes.

Jonas pulls away from our kiss and looks fiercely at Josh, his nostrils flaring, daring him to contradict whatever statement he's just made with that kiss. When Josh doesn't speak, Jonas does.

"One can easily forgive a child who's afraid of the dark. The real tragedy of life is when men are afraid of the light," he says, his chest heaving.

Chapter 4
Sarah

"Wow, Sarah, what the hell just happened?" Kat asks.

We're sitting on Jonas' balcony overlooking the twinkling lights of the Seattle skyline, drinking wine and finishing the sushi rolls Jonas ordered for us earlier. Josh and Jonas are inside, either talking or beating the crap out of each other. It's not clear which. And I can't stop thinking about that "let me show you what she means to me" kiss Jonas planted on my lips a few moments ago in front of Kat and Josh. Day-am. That was quite a kiss. Wooh! If that's how crazy kisses, then keep bringing the crazy, baby. Please and thank you.

"Oh, Kat, there's so much I've got to tell you."

"Let's start with what the hell Jonas was doing to you in his bedroom earlier. Holy Fornication, Batman! I didn't try to hear, I promise—but it was unavoidable. He was either giving you the best damned orgasm of your life or murdering you—it sounded like you were dying a gruesome death in there." She laughs.

Of all the word choices... Good Lord. "Oh my God, Kat, never, ever say anything like that around Jonas. *Please.*" I feel sick at the thought.

Kat's eyes go wide. "Why?"

I tell Kat about the horrific trauma of Jonas' childhood—about my poor, sweet Jonas witnessing his mother's savage rape and murder as he watched from her closet, and how he's blamed himself for her death ever since—with the cruel encouragement of his father.

"Oh my God," Kat says softly. "That's horrible." Kat looks like she feels physically ill. "Wow."

"And on top of that, his father killed himself when Josh and Jonas were seventeen."

"Oh no."

"And his dad left a suicide note that in some way blamed Jonas for everything."

Kat is silent for a long moment. "Well, that sheds a whole new light on Jonas' freak-out in there."

"Yup."

Kat's thinking. "So Josh wasn't there when his mom was killed? Just Jonas?"

"Just Jonas." I exhale. Even talking about this stuff makes me ache all over.

"So judging by the conversation in there, that must be a 'thing' between them—'You weren't there, I was.' Maybe some unresolved stuff?"

I nod. "I can't imagine how their mother's murder has messed them both up—plus their dad, too. Ugh. So horrible."

"Ugh," Kat agrees. She takes a long sip of her wine. "Obviously, Jonas got the worst of it, but God only knows what kind of head-trip Josh has gone through his whole life, too—maybe some kind of weird survivor's guilt or something?" She sips her wine again.

She's so right. I hadn't thought about Josh's journey in all this.

"Talk about a mind fuck for both of them," Kat says. "Just growing up without a mom is tough enough, but add the rest on top of that, too . . ."

I sigh. I feel ill.

"Well," Kat exhales loudly. "Let's talk about something happy now, shall we?"

"Yes, let's."

We clink glasses.

"Here's a happy thought," she says. "Jonas sure has an interesting book collection."

I look at her quizzically.

"I went into his office to use his computer and wound up taking a little tour of his book shelf. *How to Blow Her Mind.* That one looked interesting. *Female Orgasm: Unlocking the Mystery.* Oh, and my favorite: *Becoming a Sexual Samurai: Mastering the Art of Making Love.*" She laughs. "Some interesting reading."

I blush.

"You think Jonas might let me borrow some of his books? I

think my next boyfriend should study them thoroughly and take a final exam."

I can't help but smile broadly. "Jonas firmly believes in striving for excellence in all he does."

"Oh, yeah? He *firmly* believes in excellence, does he?"

I giggle and roll my eyes. "Jeez, I walked right into that one."

"As usual." She chuckles at me.

We both take long sips of our wine, grinning from ear to ear.

"So what do you think of Josh?" I ask, looking at her sideways. "From what I could see, you two were like boom goes the dynamite."

Kat twists her mouth but doesn't speak.

"He's exactly your type, Kat."

"I know." She smirks. "*Exactly*. I must say, the guy is hot. But that whole thing about him joining The Club and how much he obviously *enjoyed* it . . ." She makes a face like she's sniffing a dirty diaper. "It was a tad bit Douchey McDoucheypants for my taste."

"Well, Jonas joined The Club, and he's not a douche."

"Well, yeah, as it turns out. But he *was* a bit of a douche at first, you have to admit."

I purse my lips. "No. Jonas was never a douche. He was a cocky-bastard-motherfucker, but never a douche."

"Oh, thanks for the clarification." She shrugs. "Who knows, maybe Josh will turn out to be like Jonas—a knight in shining armor disguised as a cocky-bastard-motherfucker. Or maybe he'll just turn out to be a cocky-bastard-motherfucker disguised as a douche." She sighs loudly.

"I like Josh. He's got a big heart. He dropped everything when Jonas called and said he needed him—no questions asked."

"That true." She smiles. "And I must admit, now that I know about his horrible childhood, I do so desperately want to *fix* him."

"Oh boy. Good luck with that." I sip my wine.

"Hey, you never know—I could be The One Girl in the Whole World Who Can Fix Him. It sure looks like you've fixed Jonas."

"Ha! Oh yeah, as you just now so plainly witnessed, Jonas is totally, completely fixed." I pat my palms together. "My work here is done."

She laughs.

I sigh. "Jonas still has a long way to go to be cured of all that ails him, I do believe. But so do I. We're undertaking a mutual effort."

Kat smashes her lips together, genuinely touched. "I like that."

I bite my lip. I've never said anything like that out loud about any man. But it's true. We're fixing each other.

Kat takes a bite of a spicy tuna roll. "Josh is definitely hot, though, I will say that."

"You're dying of curiosity about him, admit it."

Kat takes another bite of sushi. She shrugs. "Maybe."

"Maybe?" I laugh. "It's written all over your face. You're *dying.*"

She laughs. "I'd sure like to know what the hell he was going to say about his application—"

"Oh my God, I know!"

"He was just about to say what he requested," Kat squeals.

"And then he just shut his mouth and stopped talking all of a sudden."

"Mid-sentence!'"

"And looked *right* at you, Kat."

Kat shrieks with laughter. "I was like... yes?... and?... what?... *Yes?* You requested *what* in your application, Josh?" Kat throws her head back, howling with laughter.

"I wanted to scream at the top of my lungs when he didn't finish that sentence."

"Me, too." Kat's laughing so hard she's crying. "I was peeing." She wipes her eyes and exhales. "Oh, Sarah, we're so bad."

"*We're* not bad—*I'm* bad. He's not *your* boyfriend's brother. I can't be wondering this stuff about Josh—surely, I'm going to hell."

"Ah, so Jonas is your boyfriend now? It's official?"

I nod, blushing.

Kat nudges my shoulder. "Awesome, girl."

I'm suddenly too flooded with happiness to reply. I still can't believe he's all mine.

Kat pauses, apparently deciding what to say. "He seems pretty intense, though, Sarah," she finally says. Her tone has shifted. She's warning me. She's wary. "He's not exactly the happy-go-lucky type."

I shrug. Perhaps not. But she hasn't seen what I've seen. She hasn't seen Jonas scale a thirty-foot waterfall like he was climbing a step stool. She hasn't seen him bite my ass (literally) and hoot with glee about getting to lick his baby's sweet pussy. She hasn't seen him laugh until he cried over something silly I've said. He sure seemed pretty happy-go-lucky during all those moments. And, anyway, happy-go-lucky isn't everything. She wouldn't question him if she'd seen the way he cried in my arms when he told me about his mother, or the way he looked when he held his matching friendship bracelet up to mine and told me we're a perfect match.

"He told me he loves me," I say quietly.

"Really?" She's shocked. She wasn't expecting that at all. "In Belize?"

"Mmm hmm."

"Wow. He said 'Sarah, I love you?'"

I hesitate. "Well, no—not in those exact words."

Her face falls.

"It's complicated. *He's* complicated. But trust me, he told me."

She looks skeptical. And I don't blame her. Last Kat heard, Jonas was Seattle's King of the Man-Whores—with Stacy the Faker one night and me the next. She knows he took me to Belize on a whirlwind trip, of course, but she probably thinks we enjoyed some light-hearted fun in the sun. How could she ever understand what transpired between us down there—how our very souls grabbed ahold of each other? I can barely understand it myself. I'm sure she's worried I'm just another one of Jonas' many conquests—a passing distraction.

"Well, what exactly did he say to you?"

I sigh. There's no way to explain what Jonas said and did in Belize, how he bared himself to me so completely—and how he finally got me to let go and surrender myself to him in ways I've never done before. It's all too personal, anyway.

"Just trust me," I say.

She frowns. She's not at all convinced.

"He told me," I mutter. "Even if he didn't say the magic words."

She nods, but I feel like she's humoring me.

I sigh. She just doesn't understand. Jonas told me his feelings the best way he knows how, and that's enough for me. I love him, even if he can't or won't say, "I love you," even if he *never* says those exact words. When it comes to Jonas, I don't need conventional. I don't need usual. I don't need happy-go-lucky. I just need him.

The hard part, though, I must admit, is not letting those damned words slip out of my own mouth. Every time I look into his mournful eyes, every time I touch his taut skin, every time he makes love to me, every time he looks lost or swallowed alive by his demons, or holds me tight out of some frantic impulse to protect me, every time he makes me climax and scream his name, I desperately want to say those words to him.

But I can't. I know I can't—no matter how powerful the urge. Because, without a doubt, if I say those particular words to Jonas Faraday, they'll scare the bajeezus out of him and blast our nascent relationship to Kingdom Come. I know it without a doubt. And I'm fine with that. I really am. We're mutually stricken with a serious mental disease—madness—something better and deeper and hotter and more beautiful than anything I've ever experienced before. And that's enough. We don't need three clichéd little words to make our love official. We just need each other.

All of a sudden, I can't stand to be apart from him.

I stand, looking at my watch. It's already close to one o'clock. This has been the longest day of my life—I woke up in frickin' Belize this morning, for Pete's sake. I stretch my arms above my head. Back to reality. I've got class tomorrow, homework to do. Study outlines to get from my study group. Oh shit, I've got to find a new job. Damn. And I can't manage any of that without a good night's sleep—not to mention without a laptop or textbooks or any of the clothes from my apartment. But I'll figure all that out in the morning. Right now I want one thing. Jonas Faraday. Inside me.

"Come on," I say to Kat. "Let's go back inside."

Jonas and Josh are sitting on the couch, talking calmly. Good sign.

Without a word, I waltz across the living room, right up to Jonas. I pull him up off the couch, press my body against his, take his face in my hands, and kiss him deeply.

"You take such good care of me," I breathe into him. "Thank you."

There's no better way to tell Kat what Jonas means to me than to show her. If she doesn't believe Seattle's King of the Man-Whores has fallen desperately in love with me, if she doesn't understand the depth of our emotional connection, if she can't see the goodness radiating off him, the kindness, the beauty, that's her problem, not mine. I know who he is and how he feels about me.

"You're welcome," Jonas says quietly. His face is on fire. He leans in and kisses me again—Kat and Josh be damned. When his tongue enters my mouth, my entire body sizzles with electricity. I can feel his erection nudging against me. Good thing, because I've got my own girlie version of an erection throbbing inside my panties, too.

"Have you two made nice?" I ask.

Jonas nods.

"You've come up with a plan to conquer the world?"

Jonas shakes his head in a "yes and no" kind of way. "Sort of," he breathes into my lips. "But Rome wasn't built in a day." He leans down and lifts me up by my hips, making me gasp, and slings me over his shoulder like a caveman. "We'll just have to finish plotting world domination at breakfast." He bounds out of the living room toward his bedroom, my head dangling and bobbing down his broad back as he goes.

"Don't worry about me; I'm fine," Josh calls after us. "I'll just party the night away with Party Girl with a Hyphen."

"Oh no, you won't. I'm going to sleep, Playboy," Kat replies, her voice just barely within earshot as Jonas closes in on his bedroom door. "You'll have to find another Mickey Mouse roller coaster to ride tonight."

Chapter 5
Jonas

I fling her down onto my bed, cue up "Dangerous" by Big Data, and rip her clothes off without mercy. After tearing my own clothes off, too, I sit on the edge of my bed, hard as a rock, and wordlessly beg her to fuck some serenity into me. With a low moan, she straddles me, encircling her legs tightly behind my back, and takes my full length into her. I pull her close, right up against me, and kiss her and kiss her and kiss her, staring into those big brown eyes of hers, reveling in her as my body melds into hers. We don't speak—there's no need—except, of course, for the times I moan her name, which can't be helped.

As Big Data swirls around us, I fuck her slowly, intensely, quietly, filling every inch of her, positioning my cock right up against her G-spot deep inside her. I caress the smooth skin of her back, run my hands through her hair, lick her neck, inhale her—losing myself in her, the music, her skin, her eyes, her scent. I think about absolutely nothing except how amazing she feels and how turned on I am and how awesome Big Data is for making a song so perfectly suited to blissful fucking. I'm not even thinking about making her come, to be perfectly honest—I'm too lost in the moment.

All of a sudden, out of nowhere, she comes like a motherfucker. Holy fuck, the woman explodes like a fucking rocket.

I'm absolutely floored. It's the first time Sarah's had an orgasm through intercourse alone—no tongue, no fingertips, just my cock inside her, filling her up, hitting her G-spot, just my shaft moving in and out of her, rubbing against her clit as we move together. Just my eyes locked onto hers. Just Big Data serenading us with the perfect fucking song—the perfect song for fucking.

It's incredible. The best yet, I might even say.

Our bodies fuse together in a whole new way until I can't tell where she ends and I begin, can't distinguish her pleasure from mine, her orgasm from mine, her flesh from mine. It's like discovering a treasure chest filled with priceless jewels buried six feet under the ocean's deepest floor, when all I'd been searching for was a couple of gold coins in the sand. Fucking epic. Without even trying to, I've discovered a brand new holy grail—this. Right here. Right now.

And yet . . .

I still don't say the words to her. I *feel* them, yes, of course—and thank God for that, because there was a time in my life I truly wondered if I was sociopathic—but I don't *say* them to her. Again.

Immediately after we're done, she falls asleep next to me, exhausted and totally satisfied. The woman is practically purring against me.

But I can't fall asleep. My soul has already started whispering to itself, an unpleasant truth barreling down upon it. I lie next to her for close to an hour, awake, listening to her breathing in and out, my mind reeling. Am I hopeless? Am I incapable of surrendering myself fully to Sarah the way I keep pushing her to surrender to me? Am I a hypocrite? I've been pushing her to get out of her own way—and yet I won't budge out of mine.

And damned if I know exactly what's happening, but the next thing I know I'm making love to her again. I must have drifted off to sleep at some point, at least briefly, because I wake up and I'm inside her, spooning her from behind, fucking her, and she's so wet and warm and fluttering all around me, and... Oh my God. There's nothing like watching my baby transforming into a beautiful butterfly right before my very eyes.

Chapter 6
Sarah

Jonas and I are dining in a fancy restaurant amid a flurry of activity. An army of waiters serves us, a woman sits at my feet giving me a pedicure, an artist paints our portrait from a few feet away, some woman in a toga primps my hair, and diners clatter and chatter all around our table. All of a sudden, Jonas leaps out of his chair, swats everyone away from me like he's King Kong, rips my shimmering gown off, and pushes my naked body onto our table, right on top of our food and lit candles and goblets of red wine and cutlery (including a most unfortunately positioned fork), and begins making love to me. But as he does, he's not his actual, physical self. It's hard to explain, but, in a flash, Jonas splinters and multiplies and becomes amorphic, until he's ten disembodied poltergeists, all of them with ghost lips and magical fingers and bulging biceps and chiseled abs and erect penises—all of them simultaneously embracing me, fucking me, licking me, sucking me, fondling me, groping me, kissing me, and whispering in my ears—all of them enveloping me like a slithering cloud.

And all the while, waiters refill our fallen wine glasses until they overflow, sending warm red wine gushing across my belly and spilling into my crotch and over my clit and down my thighs and between my toes until it accumulates around us into a warm and sensuous pool. The pedicure girl begins massaging my feet with the warm red wine. The hairdresser pours the wine over my scalp until it trickles down my face. And the most titillating thing of all, the thing that turns me on the most, other than Jonas himself, is how the other diners watch us and comment on our lovemaking like they're beholding a masterpiece of performance art.

"He's the most beautiful man in the world," one woman sighs.

"Clearly, but who's *she*?" a male diner asks.

"It doesn't matter. I can't take my eyes off him," another spectator observes.

"She must be something special if he wants her."

"I'm not even looking at her. I can't take my eyes off him."

"He's playing her like a grand piano."

"He's masterful."

"I've never seen anyone do it quite like this before."

"I wish he'd do that to me."

"I wish he'd make me moan like that."

"I'm having an orgasm just watching them."

Jonas' many tongues continue flickering on me, licking up the gushing red wine, his penises penetrate my every orifice, his muscles tense and bulge and contract under my fingertips, and his lips devour and suck and lick the wine off my skin and lap it out of every sensitive fold. It's almost too much pleasure to bear, intensified by the palpable desire and envy of every person watching us.

"She's losing her mind."

"She's gonna come."

"Oh God, yes, look at her. She's on the verge."

In an instant, every one of Jonas' fractured poltergeists converges on top of me, uniting and solidifying into Jonas' actual physical form.

"I love you, Sarah," he says, looking deeply into my eyes.

"Don't leave me, Jonas."

He cups my face in his hands. They're dripping in red wine. "I'll never leave you," he says. "I love you." He lifts his head and addresses our audience. "I love her. I love Sarah Cruz."

My clit, as well as everything connected to it, begins pulsing with emphatic pleasure. It's a sensation so concentrated, so undeniable, so *subversive*, it yanks me right out of my dream and into consciousness, at which point I realize that all the delicious pulsing occurring in my dream is actually happening in real life, too, inside my physical body. Holy frickin' ecstasy, I'm having an effing orgasm in my sleep! I can't believe it—the girl who only recently thought she couldn't have an orgasm at all, under any circumstance, a self-proclaimed Mount Everest Kind of Girl—is coming all by herself, powered by nothing but her own twisted imagination. Oh. My. Gawd. And what an orgasm it is. Talk about conquering the unconquerable mountain. Holy crappola. I feel like my entire pelvis, led by my clit, is going to explode right off my body and zip around the room like an errant balloon.

When my body stops pulsing, I grope feverishly behind me for Jonas' sleeping body and press my naked backside into him. Quickly, urgently, I stroke him into hardness (which isn't difficult to do), and, even before he's fully awakened, I slip his full length inside me and ride him rhythmically, reaching between my legs to feel him slipping in and out of me, touching myself, touching him, rubbing myself against his hard shaft, moaning his name. In no time at all, his mind becomes aware of what his body is doing. His lips find my neck, his warm hands find my breasts and belly and hips and clit, his fingers slip inside my moaning mouth, and his movement inside me deepens and intensifies.

I close my eyes as the pleasure inside me escalates and fills me to bursting. I remember him lapping at the red wine from the sensitive folds of my skin, how the envious diners watched us—and, most of all, how Jonas proclaimed, "I love Sarah Cruz" loud enough for everyone to hear. Lo and behold, warm waves of concentrated pleasure begin warping inside me again, emanating from my epicenter, making my body tighten and clench and release and contract around Jonas' erection.

His arms embrace me from behind and I clutch them around me, moving my body with his, coaxing him to his climax. But, much to my surprise, he pulls out of me, pushes me onto my back, and begins pleasuring me in every conceivable way. He kisses my breasts and neck and face and runs his hands over my thighs and sucks on my fingers and toes and kisses my inner thighs, and, finally, laps at me with his warm and magical tongue, licking my sweet spot with particular fervor—and in record time, I come *again*, this time like I'm exploding and melting at the same time. Holy banana cream pie, how sweet it is.

When I stop writhing and moaning, I can't move. He turns my lifeless form onto my belly and rides his happy, exhausted, horny little pony until he comes, too. And, I'll be damned, when he does, against all odds, I pulse and seize and vibrate yet again, right along with him. Not with eyes-rolling-back-into-my-head intensity, mind you—I'm too far gone for that—but, rather, like I'm his go-kart and he's just revved the engine one final, shriek-inducing time.

And now we're done, both of us completely spent.

He presses against me, holding me from behind.

And I'm a wet noodle. A sweaty wet noodle. A satisfied, sweaty wet noodle. I can't move a single muscle. And I can't speak, either. My vocal chords are non-functional—a couple of useless mucous membranes inside my throat.

Wow. Wow. Wow.

Mind officially blown.

Un-fricking-believable. Incredible. Delicious.

Can I get a woot woot from myself?

Woot woot!

If I could speak, which I can't, I'd scream from the top of every mountain right now: "I'm officially a sex kitten, peeps! I'm *multi-orgasmic*, bitches! Boom!"

I stretch myself out against his body and feel myself slipping into total relaxation. I've never felt quite like this before, so fulfilled, so satisfied—and so frickin' powerful, too. Tonight, I'm reborn, for the second time in my life—the prior time being that magical night in Belize when Mount Everest first toppled—and it's all thanks to this hunky-monkey-magic-man boyfriend of mine, Mr. Fuck Wizard himself. Mr. Most Beautiful Man I've Ever Seen. Mr. Heart as Big as the Grand Canyon. Mr. Sad Eyes. Mr. Tortured Soul. Mr. Divine Original. Mr. Manly Man-ness-y Manly Man.

Mr. Jonas Faraday.

My sweet Jonas.

Oh God, how I love this man.

I close my eyes. My mind yawns and instantly begins drifting into blackness . . .

"Sarah," Jonas whispers, and my mind lurches back to full attention. Something in his voice makes me think he's about to say something important. "Sarah, I . . ." The hairs on the back of my neck stand up, anticipating what he's about to say. He pauses a really long time—an excruciating amount of time—but he doesn't finish his thought.

He inhales sharply and his tone shifts direction. "My

Magnificent Sarah," he finally says, stroking the curve of my hip. "Are you awake?" he whispers.

"Mmm hmm." Barely.

"That was a nice wake-up call."

I touch his hand on my hip. He grabs my hand and squeezes it.

"I had a dream that made me a wee bit horny," I mumble softly.

"Apparently. What did you dream about?"

"You. Making love to you. I had an orgasm in the dream, and then I woke up and I was actually having an orgasm."

His breathing halts in surprise. "Oh, wow." He presses himself into me and runs his hands over my belly.

I turn onto my opposite side and face him. "Before you, I thought there was something wrong with me. I thought I was born without some magic button everyone else has."

He inhales deeply, like he's trying to calm himself. He brushes a hair away from my face. But he doesn't speak.

"And now look at me. I'm kicking ass and taking names—I'm a sexual superhero."

He puts on a low movie-announcer voice. "They call her... *Orgasma*." He smiles and nuzzles his nose into mine. "Orgasma the All-Powerful."

I mimic his announcer voice. "Able to leap tall cocks in a single bound."

"No." He's stern. "Able to leap one and only one tall *cock* in a single bound. Only mine."

"Well, of course." I roll my eyes. "That's the biggest 'duh' of the century, Jonas."

He laughs. He nuzzles my nose again.

"You big dummy," I add.

He shoots me a crooked half-smile. "I just wanted to be clear about that."

"Got it."

We lie in the dark, staring at each other for a moment. I can't remember ever feeling this happy before.

"Thank you," I say simply. "Thank you for helping me discover my magic button. I don't feel like I'm defective anymore. I feel powerful."

He kisses me gently. "You are powerful."

"I had no idea sex could feel so good. You really are good at this."

"No, I'm fucking awesome at this, I told you. But I can't take all the credit. Your body is *designed* to do exactly what it did tonight—get off again and again and again. It's not magic—women don't need a refractory period after orgasm the way men do."

"Refractory period?"

"A period of recovery. Women don't need to recover after orgasm—they can climax again and again, almost instantly after the first time, as long as they get the right stimulation."

I'm blown away. "Are you sure? I always thought some small percentage of women were multi-orgasmic, like porn stars or whatever, and a small percentage of women on the other end of the spectrum can't come at all, and then everyone else falls somewhere in the middle."

"Nah, that's a myth. All women are *designed* to come over and over. Just because most women haven't accomplished it—because they don't know how to do it, don't know it's possible, their boyfriends suck at sex, they've never masturbated and figured out what gets them off, whatever—it doesn't mean they're not *built* to do it. All the parts are there, even if they don't know how to use them."

His eyes are so animated when he talks about this stuff. I could fall asleep at the drop of a hat right now, and he's just getting more and more excited as we talk.

"Your first orgasm is like priming the pump," he continues, fully awake. "The first one might take a while, as we've discovered, my little Mount Everest, but once you're there, once you've reached the peak, your body is ready to do it again and again if you keep yourself open. And the great thing is, it's much easier to get there the second and third times."

I shake my head. Why does he know more about my own sexuality than I do? Why has no one ever told me any of this stuff?

"At the end of the day, female orgasm is always about your head—getting rid of your psychological hang-ups. After you get off the first time, you've just gotta keep your mind open and get the right stimulation—from someone who knows how—and you'll be off to the races every time."

"From *someone* who knows how?"

"Well, from *me*, of course—fuck, don't misunderstand that part. Let me be perfectly clear, yet again: Only from *me*. Always me."

I smile at him. "Jonas Faraday."

"The one and only."

"The sexual samurai."

He laughs. "Ah, you've seen my book collection."

"No, Kat did. She wants to make all your books required reading for her next boyfriend."

He chuckles. "Well, a guy can *read* about this stuff all he wants, but if he doesn't have some God-given talent to start with, it's pointless. It's like being a musician—you can be classically trained to play all the right notes, but no one can teach you to *feel* the music with your soul. Muddy Waters *felt* the music. Bob Dylan *felt* the music. No one can learn how to do that—it's true artistry."

"Ah, so you're a sexual *arteest*, are you?"

He squeezes me. "I am. And you're my canvas." He kisses my neck and grabs my ass at the same time.

"I'll be your canvas any time, big boy."

He's thinking about something. "My whole life, I've had this innate *understanding*. It's like this weird empathy; I don't know what else to call it." He pauses. "I've never told anyone this . . ."

I wait. There's absolutely nothing better than a sentence that starts with, "I've never told anyone this . . ."

"It started when I was little. My mother used to get these horrible headaches, and I was the only one who could make them go away, just by massaging her head the right way . . ." He stops talking.

"It's okay," I finally say. "Tell me."

He shakes his head.

"Tell me, baby. I'm listening."

He shifts internal gears. Clearly, there will be no more talking about his mother. "When I touch you, or fuck you, or taste you—oh fuck, I'm turning myself on again, baby—" He kisses me deeply, his hands firmly on my ass again. "*Albóndigas,*" he whispers. *Meatballs.*

I laugh. "*Siempre tus albóndigas.*" *Always your meatballs.*

He smiles at me.

"Tell me," I coax him.

"When I fuck you or taste you or touch you, whatever, it's like I can *feel* what you're feeling—I mean, like, literally *feel* it, you know?

57

And, holy fuck, it gets me off." He grunts, obviously imagining whatever sensation he's talking about.

"I told you—you're a woman wizard, baby. You've got magical, mystical powers."

He sighs and touches my cheek. "I can't wait to keep exploring the depths of you, Sarah Cruz. You're a vast and uncharted ocean, you know that?" He pauses. "You're *my* ocean."

I'm filled with the sudden urge to tell him I love him. He's better than any dream. He makes me feel safe. He makes me feel loved. He makes me feel *good*—so, so, so *frickin'* good. He makes me feel special. I love him. And, oh my God, I want to tell him, in exactly those words.

But, nope. I can't. No way. It's a non-starter.

And that's okay. *I'm his ocean,* he says. Not too shabby. It's enough. It really is.

"Yet again, you're a poet," I whisper.

"Only with you."

He wraps his arms around me and squeezes me. "Sarah . . .," he whispers, "I . . ." He clears his throat. But he doesn't say anything more.

I can feel myself drifting off to sleep. Whatever else he's going to say, it will have to wait until morning.

"Madness," I whisper. And then I close my eyes and slip into a deep and blissful sleep.

Chapter 7
Jonas

Thinking is just the soul talking with itself, or so Plato says. If that's true, then for the last few hours, while everyone else in the house has been fast asleep, my soul's been chatting up a fucking storm with itself. It's okay, though, because while my soul's been pontificating its ass off, my body's been getting shit done.

I washed and ironed Sarah's clothes from her suitcase (all of which were covered in Belizian mud and mosquito repellant). I worked out like a demon (powered by Rx Bandit's awesome new album). I went to Whole Foods and picked up breakfast for everyone (organic berries and Greek yogurt and zucchini-quinoa muffins). I went through my emails (and ignored every one of them except those pertaining to my new rock climbing gyms). I registered and loaded the laptops I bought for Sarah and Kat (which, thanks to my assistant, were delivered to my house first thing this morning). Bringing order and clarity to my environment has allowed me to bring order and clarity to my mind, too—and now, I'm pretty confident about my strategy going forward.

When I first opened Sarah's suitcase and smelled Belize wafting off her clothes, I wanted to charge into my bedroom, scoop up her sleeping body, and whisk her straight back to paradise. Fuck real life. Fuck The Club. Fuck being back in Seattle with Kat and Josh and work and school. But then I thought about what happened in my bedroom late last night (or, technically, early this morning), right here in the paradise of my bedroom, and I quickly forgot all about abducting Sarah back to Belize.

I look out my kitchen window. The sun is rising, illuminating not only my countertops with its soft golden light, but my consciousness, too, suddenly making it impossible for me to ignore a despicable truth: I'm incapable of uttering those three little words to anyone. Even to Sarah.

I sigh.

Before last night, I thought I'd been holding off saying those magic words for twenty-three long years because my soul knew it could only say them in the presence of pure *woman-ness*. I thought I'd reserved saying those words since the age of seven because my soul innately understood I would one day say them to one woman only, the goddess and the muse, Sarah Cruz—the ideal form of woman. But last night in the dark, lying next to her after making love to her in the most intense and mind blowing and intimate ways possible, I realized I'd been making excuses for my emotional limitations all along and that, in truth, I'm fundamentally incapable of surrendering myself to the extent necessary to say those words out loud. Even to My Magnificent Sarah.

What else can I possibly conclude? If those words didn't escape my lips when my baby's body seized and convulsed from nothing but the pleasure of my body filling hers, or when she came in her sleep simply because she'd had a *dream* about me, or when she climaxed over and over for the first time in her life, finally figuring out how to harness her body's greatest power, if all of that wasn't enough to make those three words spring involuntarily from my mouth, then, clearly, I'll never fucking say them.

It pains me to admit that to myself. I want to say those words to her, I really do. But, obviously, I'm too fucked up to accomplish it. I've come a long way thanks to Sarah, but, apparently, there's only so far I can travel on broken legs. No matter what, it seems there's always going to be a non-traversable wasteland inside of me, a bastion of fuckeduppedness just beyond my conscious borders that can't be reached or breached, no matter how beautiful or earnest or amazing the woman who's trying to guide me there. I just have to accept that there are dark, untouchable places inside of me, and adjust accordingly. If I can't say the words to her, okay, I can't. It means I have to work that much harder to *show* her how I feel about her.

And that starts right now.

I flip open my laptop and create a new document—a spreadsheet entitled, "How I'm Going to Fuck The Club Up the Ass."

It's time to show my baby exactly how I feel about her. It's time to show her I can't live without her. It's time to focus on the task at hand and quit fucking around.

Human behavior flows from three sources: desire, emotion, and knowledge. Obviously, when it comes to protecting Sarah, I've got the first two elements in spades, but I'm distinctly lacking in the third category. I need to acquire some knowledge. And fast. I type out what I know about The Club onto my spreadsheet, add what I don't know, and then sit and brainstorm every methodology I can think of—good, bad, and even just plain ridiculous—for obtaining the information I currently lack.

Last night with Josh, I acted like a fucking lunatic, not to mention an asshole. I know that. I just let my emotions get the best of me. I was pissed as hell at what I perceived to be Josh's lack of loyalty and understanding of the situation, and I let that unfair perception jumble and merge with all the bullshit (real and imagined) years of therapy was supposed to fix (but apparently didn't). But this morning, after my soul's lengthy conversation with itself, not to mention some serenity-inducing fuckery with Sarah last night, I'm feeling more receptive to what Josh said.

Plato says, "Better a little that is well done, than a great deal imperfectly." And, actually, I think that's all Josh was trying to tell me last night, however inarticulately. I think he was trying to say The Club is a huge beast of a mountain to climb, and that if I approach climbing it haphazardly, I won't gain any traction and might even cause an avalanche. What I have to do is develop an effective plan of attack and execute it with supreme and careful excellence. There's too much at stake to do otherwise. What I need to do is frame my mission as "protecting Sarah (and Kat)"—rather than "decimating The Club."

Those two concepts *might* be one and the same—you never know—but they might not be. Right now, I don't have enough information to reach a sound conclusion on the issue one way or another. If destroying The Club turns out to be a component of protecting Sarah, then fuck yeah, that's what I'll do, and gladly. But if something short of that turns out to be a more effective option, then I'll have to be man enough to put my dick away and do whatever's going to achieve my mission. This is not the time to swing my dick around just for the hell of it. This is the time to protect my baby with maximum *effectiveness*.

And it all starts with gathering some knowledge.

"Good morning." It's Kat.

I look up from my screen. "Hi."

"Is Sarah up yet?"

"No, still sleeping like a baby. Same with Josh." Kat's dressed for work. She's got her purse on her shoulder. She's holding her rolling suitcase. "You're leaving?"

"Yeah, I've got to get to work. It turns out Mondays are considered workdays by my boss. Who knew?"

"You think that's wise?"

"I don't have a choice—I've got to work."

I don't respond.

"And, yeah. I think it's wise. I was totally freaked out yesterday, kind of in shock, but today I realize I can't live in fear. I've just got to live my life."

"Have you told Sarah you're leaving?"

"No. I haven't seen her this morning. I texted her."

"How about I put you up in a hotel," I begin. "Maybe just until we have a better grasp of what's going on—"

"No, I'm good. That's nice of you to offer, though. Thanks."

I'd like to keep close tabs on Kat, at least until I've got a better understanding of what I'm up against here. But, hey, she's an adult. Now, if she were my girlfriend, there's no fucking way I'd let her walk out that door right now—but she's not my girlfriend. And, anyway, I'm guessing The Club's real focus, if they have one at all— who the fuck knows what they're thinking?—is Sarah.

I give Kat the laptop I bought for her. Her eyes bug out of her head in surprise, but she nonetheless politely says she can't accept it, blah, blah, fucking blah. I appreciate her politeness, of course, but I don't have time to play "wow, we've both got such great manners" this morning. I've got too much to do.

"Kat, take the computer. Please. Help me alleviate my guilty conscience for putting this whole situation in motion. *I insist*." In my vast experience with women, "I insist" is the magic phrase that ends all polite pushback regarding gifts and money and who's paying for dinner. It's the ultimate trump card a man holds over a woman. It never fails.

She acquiesces, right on cue. "Well, okay. Thank you so much."

"And I've arranged a cleaning service to come to your place. If your apartment looks anything like Sarah's did, you're definitely going to need some help."

Again, she half-heartedly goes through the social nicety of refusing me until I insist and make her shut the fuck up.

I have a sudden thought. "You know what? I'm gonna hire a bodyguard for you for at least a couple days—"

"No, that's... excessive, isn't it? You can't do that."

"It's not up for debate. I'll email you the information—and the guy's picture—so when he introduces himself, you'll know he's exactly who he claims to be. Just for a few days, Kat. Humor me."

She purses her lips.

"I *insist*. Just while I figure this out, okay? If you don't let me do that for you, then I'll worry about you—and I can't afford the distraction of worrying about you."

She smirks at me. "You're good at that."

"At what?"

"At getting what you want."

I shrug. It's true. So what?

"Thank you, Jonas. For everything. Tell Sarah I'll call her later."

"Will do. Hey, take a muffin with you. You gotta eat."

She grabs a muffin. "Thanks." She begins rolling her bag toward the door. She stops. "You know . . ."

I look up from my computer.

"You might not realize this, but Sarah doesn't normally let her guard down like she has with you—and definitely not so quickly."

I stare at her.

Kat exhales. "I just want to make sure you understand she's not just 'having fun' with you. She thinks this is something serious."

I don't speak. Clearly, she thinks I'm a flaming asshole—the asshole she saw with Stacy the Faker, I presume.

"Sarah always says I've got a heart of gold—but I don't. She's the one who wants to save the world, not me. She's the one who sees good in everyone—not me." She squints at me, clearly implying Sarah foolishly sees undeserved goodness in me. "Trust me, I'm not nearly as nice as she is."

I take this last comment to mean Kat's going to break my legs if

I hurt her best friend. I suddenly like Kat a lot.

"She's fallen hard for you, Jonas," Kat says quietly.

This isn't news to me. I already know Sarah's fallen hard for me—she's told me so herself. And, even more importantly, she's shown me so herself. Regardless, though, it feels supremely awesome to hear her best friend confirm that fact, too.

Kat shifts her weight. "I probably shouldn't tell you this, but you need to understand the situation." She takes a deep breath. "She's in love with you." She waits a beat, letting that supposedly shocking revelation wash over me. "And she thinks you're in love with her, too." She grits her teeth—or is she baring them? It's hard to say.

Again, I don't speak.

"Don't crush her, Jonas."

Wow, that last line was delivered with some serious menace. Looks like Sarah's got a best friend who's as fierce as she is. Kat is now officially golden in my book.

"Got it," I say.

She stares at me, obviously annoyed. I guess she was expecting me to say something different.

"Thanks for the heads up," I add lamely.

I like Kat—she's clearly a fantastic friend to Sarah—but my feelings for Sarah are none of her fucking business. There's only room for two—for Sarah and me—in our little cocoon built for two. I don't give a fuck about anyone's opinion of me but Sarah's.

When it's clear I've said all I'm going to say, Kat clears her throat. "Well, thanks again for the computer," she finally says.

"But it doesn't buy your trust, huh?"

She smirks. "Hell no."

"Good."

Her smirk turns into a genuine smile. "Well, okay, then."

"Okay."

She grabs the handle of her suitcase again. "Tell Playboy goodbye for me. Maybe he and I can hang out one of these days—whenever he's done chasing Mickey Mouse roller coasters, if ever."

I return her smile. "I'll tell him you said exactly that."

"Wonderful."

She starts rolling her suitcase toward the door.

"Kat, I think you're forgetting one important thing."

She stops and looks at me, her eyes blazing with pre-emptive defiance. Apparently, she's expecting some sort of knight-in-shining-armor rebuttal from me—and she's already decided that, whatever it is, it's total bullshit.

"Sarah and I picked you up in a limo yesterday, remember? How were you planning to get to work?"

Her face falls. "Oh."

The defeated look on her face makes me smirk. "Let me call a car for you."

Chapter 8

Jonas

"Okay, let's talk action items," Josh says, taking a bite of a zucchini-quinoa muffin. "What the fuck is this?"

"Zucchini-quinoa."

Josh rolls his eyes and puts the muffin down. "Why can't you ever eat anything normal?"

I ignore him and study my spreadsheet. Josh has been helping me brainstorm leads and strategies for the last twenty minutes. Sarah's still asleep, not surprisingly—we were up 'til the wee hours together, discovering Sarah's newfound orgasmic superpowers. Good God, that woman is my crack. *Orgasma.* I can't help but smile.

"All right," I say, looking at my computer screen. "Item one. You and I will forward your hacker guy whatever emails we both still have from The Club."

"Yup. Though I doubt that will yield anything."

"Worth a try."

"One would think they'd be smart enough to use dummies or encrypt their emails or insert fakers, but they might be epically stupid, you never know. And my hacker buddy is really good, so, hey, it's worth a shot."

"Who is this hacker, anyway?"

"A buddy of mine from college. He's solid, trust me—he's helped out a bunch of my friends on the down low with some pretty big stuff."

I instantly wonder why Josh's flashy friends have required the services of a top-notch hacker, but it doesn't matter—if Josh trusts this guy completely, then so do I.

"Action item two," I say. "I engage them in some sort of email exchange. Hopefully, I can get something that helps the hacker and leads us to a power player."

"Good. What are you gonna say to them?"

I consider briefly. "I could thank them for allowing me to partake in their lovely intake agent. I'll tell them she was a thoroughly enjoyable surprise—but that I'm all done with her now, thank you very much, and looking forward to the rest of my membership experience. I'll ask for assurances from the top that my intake-agent detour won't disrupt my membership in any way."

Josh twists his mouth. "That makes you sound like such an asshole. You've had your fun with their intake agent and now you're just tossing her aside?"

I shrug. "Yeah."

Josh raises his eyebrows. "After all the effort it took to find her?"

"They don't know the lengths I went to find her. For all they know, Sarah just picked up the phone and called me after our first emails. Actually, come to think of it, maybe they're not sure if Sarah and I even connected in person. Maybe they think Sarah and I emailed back and forth, she went to spy on me at my first check-in, saw me with the purple prostitute, and that was that. That would be a reasonable conclusion, wouldn't it?"

"Maybe under normal circumstances, but... Come on." He motions to me, as if my mere Jonas-ness somehow makes my hypothetical impossible.

I roll my eyes at him. "Whatever. Either way, they've read my application, so me being a gigantic asshole is exactly what they'd expect."

"You could make it sound like you thought Sarah was part of your membership. Maybe that'd make it more believable that you'd turn and burn her so damned fast."

Josh truly has no idea what I've been doing for the past year?

"Josh, they won't have trouble believing I'd turn and burn her, trust me."

He grimaces.

"Oh really, Mr. Mickey Mouse Roller Coaster? The mere thought is distasteful to your gentle sensibilities?"

He laughs. "The roller coaster thing was an *analogy*, bro—it's not necessarily my life philosophy. As a matter of fact, when I find a roller coaster I particularly like, I prefer to ride it over and over again, exclusively."

"Okay, this is getting gross. Don't talk to me about 'riding' anything ever again, motherfucker. You're making me want to puke."

"It's an *analogy*."

"It's gross. I don't need that visual of you." I shudder.

He shrugs. "I have no idea what you're talking about. I'm just talking about riding roller coasters."

"Anyway, there's no way they'd believe I thought Sarah was some sort of Club offering. They've got her computer. They've seen our emails. It's clear we both knew she was breaking the rules—I kept assuring her I wouldn't tell them she'd contacted me."

"Aha! Now it all makes sense. I've been wondering why you went ballistic about her sight unseen like that. She was the proverbial *forbidden fruit*."

"Gee, Dr. Freud, you're so fucking smart."

Except that he's wrong. Josh doesn't have a clue why I lost my shit over Sarah's first email to me—and I'll never tell him because it's none of his business. But, holy fuck, what an email it was. *A Mount Everest kind of girl like me,* she called herself. I still get tingles just thinking about it—and about how many delicious times I've climbed and conquered my beautiful Mount Everest since then.

"I like the part about you saying you're eager to move on with your membership," Josh says. "It makes it seem like Sarah never told you their dirty little secret—or, if she did, like you don't care. Either way, a good thing."

A thought is niggling at me. I pause, trying to pin it down. "Are we sure about that? Does Sarah supposedly not telling me what she discovered help or hurt the situation?"

"How could it do anything but help? If she didn't tell you, then they'll assume she's discreet. Maybe they'll decide to trust her and leave her alone."

"But what if it goes the other way? What if they think she just hasn't had the opportunity to tell me yet? Or she hasn't worked up the nerve? Or what if they think she already told me, and I didn't give a shit, and now she's pissed as hell and about to go on a rampage? Even if they think she hasn't blabbed, they might decide their best strategy is to strike quickly to ensure her continued silence—not to risk it, either way." I know I'm talking really fast, but I can't slow myself down. My heart is racing all of a sudden. What if those fuckers are planning to come after her right now? I have the sudden urge to bolt to my room and scoop her up and whisk her away to a faraway place.

"Hmm. I guess that depends on what kind of criminals we're dealing with here. I mean, it's just a prostitution ring, right? What makes you think they might be capable of physical violence?"

"What makes me think . . .? You mean besides the fact that they simultaneously broke into Kat and Sarah's apartments and smashed both places to bits? That's not enough for you right there?"

Josh's expression is noncommittal—apparently, no, that's not enough for him.

I'm sure my face clearly expresses my exasperation. "Don't get bogged down by the fact that it's 'just a prostitution ring.' It doesn't matter if their particular racket is prostitution, drugs, gambling, identity theft—whatever the fuck—it doesn't matter. What matters is that they're a highly organized crime syndicate with a shitload of money at stake. Do the math, Josh. This is big money. At the end of the day, the specific form of their criminal activity is irrelevant— what matters is that they're not going to let anyone, least of all a dispensable intake agent, fuck with their cash cow."

Josh lets that roll around in his head for a second. "I never thought about it that way. Hmm."

"And, on top of that, I'd bet anything their client roster is a who's who of some ultra-powerful people, too. They've got plenty of incentive to keep their members from learning the truth, through any means necessary."

Josh suddenly looks anxious. "An excellent point."

I'm getting myself all worked up. "They're sitting on a fucking powder keg, Josh. And, as far as they know, Sarah's the one holding the match."

"Shit."

My heart clangs sharply inside my chest. I'm breaking out into a sweat. "I'm just not sure which way to play it. The stakes are too high to fuck this up." I run my hand through my hair. *My Magnificent Sarah.* I can't let anything happen to her. My heart pounds like a motherfucker in my ears. "I just need more information to know what to do."

69

Josh nods. "Yeah, I see your point. It's tricky." He sighs. "I didn't really understand all that until now." He purses his lips, unsure about something. "Maybe you should just go to the police?"

"I thought about that. This isn't something for the local police—we need the feds. Is the FBI really gonna sick their anti-fraud unit all over this just because Sarah saw a hooker wearing two different colored bracelets? I'm sure they've got more pressing shit to deal with, and I need immediate action."

Josh looks anxious.

"My gut tells me to keep this under wraps until I can serve the whole thing up to them on a silver platter."

Josh nods.

"You know, if I ever do wind up blowing this thing wide open, it might not be pleasant for either of us. At the very least, it might be really embarrassing."

He shrugs. "I'm a single guy. It was one month of my life. I don't give a fuck. No one held it against Charlie Sheen when it came out he had sex with prostitutes all the time. I'll just make like Charlie Sheen and say 'Fuck you—I'm winning.'"

We both laugh.

"Yeah, I don't give a fuck, either. Fuck it."

"Uncle William would shit a brick, though."

"I know."

We both laugh again, imagining our straightlaced uncle—the polar opposite of our father in every way—finding out about our unseemly extracurricular activities.

Josh twists his mouth in apology. "I'm sorry about last night. I just didn't get it."

For some reason, hearing Josh say he finally gets what I've been trying to explain to him makes me feel like the weight of the world has lifted off me, like I'm finally not alone in all this.

"I'm sorry I blew up at you," I say. "Thanks for coming here on a moment's notice."

"Of course. I'll always come when you call, man."

I take a deep breath, panic about the situation and relief that Josh is on board crashing through my body all at once. "Okay, we'll sit on item number two for a bit—think it through some more. I won't email them directly just yet."

Josh nods. "Okay. So what's next on the list, then?"

"Item number three. Find these assholes the good old-fashioned way. We find a real person in The Club, no matter how low on the totem pole, and just keep connecting the dots all the way up until we identify someone we can fuck up the ass. And in the meantime, I keep Sarah safe and out of their crosshairs at all times."

He purses his lips. "You know, we really should ask Sarah what she thinks. She's probably got all kinds of ideas on where to start. I bet she could tell us—"

"No, I don't want Sarah involved in any of this. This is just gonna be you and me."

"Bro." Josh looks at me like I'm an idiot. "She worked for them and she's super smart. She's bound to have an idea or two—"

"I don't want Sarah involved."

Josh throws up his hands. "I'm not talking about asking her to *do* anything. I'm just saying let's ask her for *input*."

"No." It comes out louder than intended. I take another deep breath and collect myself. "You don't know Sarah like I do. If we ask her for *input*, she'll immediately start *doing* something—surveillance or research or snooping around or God knows what. She's not a sit-on-the-sidelines kind of girl. She's the one who emailed me in the first place, remember?"

Josh smiles broadly.

"Yes, granted, that part worked out well," I concede, stifling a smile of my own. That's the understatement of the year. "But the point is, she doesn't sit around thinking, 'golly gosh, wouldn't it be nice to know x y z,' she gets out there and *does* whatever the fuck she has to do to figure out x y z."

Josh sighs in exasperation. "Yeah, but—"

"When she had a question about this friend of mine—remember the time you invited that little league team to our box seats at the Mariners' game?"

Josh nods. "Of course."

"Well, after that, I became friendly with one of the kids and—"

Josh's face contorts in complete surprise.

"It's a long story—totally irrelevant. But when Sarah was curious about my friendship with the kid, what did she do? She paid a visit to his mom at her work and got all the information she wanted."

I smile. "She's such a lawyer-in-training, I swear to God. The girl is so fucking snoopy."

Josh gives me his patented laughing-at-me-with-his-eyes look.

"And before she ever agreed to meet me in person, she *spied* on me at my Club check-in—I told you about that, right? That's when I hooked up with that Purple who showed up a week later at some other guy's check-in as a fucking Yellow?"

Josh grimaces in disgust. "Yeah, you told me about that."

"And that's how the shit hit the fan in the first place—Sarah spied on me and the yellow guy, too—just because her *curiosity* got the best of her both times—and that's how Stacy the Prostitute put two and two together and ratted her out."

Josh nods.

"You see? That's Sarah. She gets *curious*—and when she does, she doesn't hesitate to do whatever the fuck she has to do to *satisfy* that curiosity. You don't know her like I do, man. She's a force of nature, that woman. When she sets her mind to something... I don't want her taking charge and hijacking things and unwittingly doing something that puts her on The Club's radar screen any more than she already is. The next time they come after her might not be a simple break-in."

"I get it. I really do, man. Okay? Don't freak out on me—I'm on board. But if we're looking for a place to start connecting the dots, I'm just saying Sarah would know better than anyone what our first dots should be. We should at least ask her."

"No. It's non-negotiable, Josh. I don't want Sarah involved. I'm gonna keep her safe through any means necessary, even if that means benching her from the game."

Josh sighs. "Jonas."

"No. I'm keeping her out of harm's way, both physical and emotional." I lower my voice. "She had a rough childhood, Josh. Her father was a bastard—an abuser." I take a measured breath, trying to calm the raging beast welling up inside of me. "Sarah said she and her mom 'escaped' him. Fucking bastard. If he were here right now, I'd tear him limb from limb."

Josh looks anguished.

"She's been scared enough times in her life. She doesn't need to deal with this kind of bullshit. She doesn't need to be scared. I just want to keep her out of it."

Josh rubs his face and exhales. He doesn't speak for a long beat. "Okay, bro," he finally concedes. "We'll do things your way."

That's exactly right—we'll do things my fucking way. I'm going to keep Sarah out of harm's way and make her feel safe and protected at all times, through any means necessary, no matter what. All my baby needs to do is go to her classes and study her law books and chase that scholarship she wants so badly and help her mom save the world one battered woman at a time and then come home to me and spread her smooth olive thighs on top of my crisp white sheets and let me glory in her and make love to her and lick her and fuck her and kiss her and suck her and show her how I feel. I want her relaxed and happy and satisfied and carefree—not sitting around thinking some boogeyman is coming to get her. And, quite selfishly, I don't want Sarah even thinking about The Club anymore, in any capacity. From now on, she can channel all her sexual curiosity into me. She's all mine now—and I want her undivided attention.

My heart pounds in my ears.

I pull my Club-issued iPhone out of my jeans pocket and toss it onto the kitchen table. "We don't need Sarah's input, anyway. I've still got the keys to their kingdom. The fuckers haven't deactivated me."

Chapter 9
Jonas

"Wow." Josh pauses briefly, staring at my Club-issued iPhone on the table. "I'm surprised they haven't cut you off. They must not be sure if you're friend or foe. Maybe you're right—maybe they don't know for sure what's gone down between you and Sarah."

"Yeah, and they'd better be goddamned positive I'm the enemy before cutting me off. Hell hath no fury like an asshole unjustly separated from his quarter of a million bucks."

Josh lets out a loud puff of air. "Oh my God, Jonas. You joined The Club for a *year?*"

Shit. I've never mentioned that little detail to Josh before. I completely forgot he assumes I joined for a fun-filled month, just like he did.

"That's hardcore, man. Damn."

He's right. I shrug.

"Ha!" He shakes his head, smiling. "I feel totally vindicated. Which Faraday brother is the playboy now?"

I can't help but laugh. Of the two of us, Josh has always been tagged as the bad boy playboy, maybe because he's always so public about his relationships and partying, when all the while it's me who's been burning through women like a lawnmower through tall grass.

"Oh, hey, that reminds me. Kat left a message for you—which she addressed specifically to 'Playboy.'"

Josh looks disappointed. "She left?"

"Yeah, she had to go to work. Said she has to 'live her life.' But she gave me a message for you: 'Tell *Playboy* I'd love to hang out with him some time—whenever he's done chasing Mickey Mouse roller coasters, if ever.'"

Josh groans.

I laugh. "Hey, man, you did it to yourself. You're the one who said all that Mickey Mouse bullshit right in front of her. Dumbass."

Josh looks totally bummed.

"You liked her, huh?"

"Did you *see* her? Oh my God."

"She's just your type."

"She's *everybody's* type."

"Well, she obviously thinks you're a total asswipe."

Josh smashes his mouth into a hard line. "She was sassy, too. I like sassy."

"It's your own damned fault."

"Fuck you. You're the one who signed up for a whole *year's* worth of Mickey Mouse roller coasters, not me. Pervert."

He's got me there. I've got no comeback.

"What the hell did you ask for in your application that you needed a whole *year* of it?" he asks.

"It doesn't matter. I told you—I was having some kind of nervous breakdown. What did you ask for in *your* application?"

"None of your business." Josh's face turns earnest. He fidgets. "Hey, man, I had no idea you were... you know, having such a hard time. I thought you were living large, being a beast. I had no idea you were... you know... "

"Turning into Dad?"

Josh's face flushes.

"It's okay. Neither did I. I'd become quite the expert at distracting myself from the truth."

Josh nods. "Turn and burn," he says quietly.

"Turn and burn," I agree. A series of images from the past year flashes through my mind. Turn and burn, indeed. "But then Sarah came along and kicked my ass, man. Holy shit, did she ever kick my ass. That woman can spot bullshit a mile a way—and she totally called me on mine."

"Sounds like she was exactly what you needed."

"She was—she *is*."

"But next time, if you're having a rough time, talk to me, okay? I never want you to... you know... feel like . . ."

"There won't be a next time."

"Just don't do something stupid."

"I won't. Never again. I promise."

"I've always got your back. You know that, right? I never want you to—"

"I won't."

Josh exhales. "I can't believe you spent a quarter million bucks on The Club—on anything, actually. It's so un-Jonas-like of you."

He's right. I don't spend money frivolously. Clearly, I was out of my mind.

"And Sarah knows you joined for a whole year?"

"Yeah, she's the one who processed my application." I sigh, suddenly wistful. *My Beautiful Intake Agent.* She had me the minute her email landed in my inbox.

"Wow. She knows all the ways you're a total pervert and she still wants you?"

I nod.

"You're a lucky bastard."

"I know."

"Does she know everything else, too? You know, about . . ." He pauses, suddenly unsure how to proceed.

I tilt my head and wait. But Josh doesn't have the heart to finish that sentence.

He swallows hard.

I finish his sentence for him. "Does she know about The Lunacy?"

Josh nods.

It suddenly occurs to me Josh is the only living person (besides doctors and therapists, of course) who knows everything about The Lunacy—the euphemism we use to refer to "the time when Jonas lost his fucking mind." There was nothing remotely funny about that period of my life, of course, nothing at all, but I've since learned that scoffing about it, calling it something as irreverent and light-hearted and dismissive as "The Lunacy," effectively minimizes the pain and relegates it to a distant and containable memory.

I've gotten quite adept at compartmentalizing that stuff into a lidded box inside me, in fact, and now that I'm sane and in control of my mind and body and soul, now that I've come to realize that my father was fallible—that he wasn't God, for fuck's sake, or the supreme arbiter of my worth as a human being, that his suicide note was just fucking *malicious* and not reflective of the objective truth—now that I've figured out how to choose serenity and enlightenment and sanity through visualizing the divine originals and striving for excellence, I'm reborn—a totally different person. I'm a man now, a fucking beast, just like Josh always says—not a mute and frozen boy in a closet or some kind of pathetic pussy-ass seeking his father's forgiveness that will never come. I'm strong now. Especially now that I've found my Sarah.

I put down the muffin I was holding. "Well, I told her about... what happened... you know, on that day when we were kids," I say quietly. The levity of our conversation has instantly vanished. He knows what day I'm talking about, of course—the day that changed both our lives forever, the day that fucked us up irreversibly, especially me. The day we've both tried, in vain, to overcome our whole lives.

Josh looks surprised. And it's no wonder—I never, ever talk about what I witnessed from the cowardly safety of my mother's closet. I've certainly never told any of my other girlfriends about it.

"I also told her about Dad—what he did. You know, just the basics, no details."

Josh nods, clenching his jaw. His eyes flash with sudden hardness.

"But I didn't tell her about... everything that happened right after that. To me."

Josh nods his agreement. "The Lunacy."

I nod. *The Lunacy*. It's my penultimate shame, second only to my life's greatest and most inexcusable disgrace—my unforgivable failure to move from that damned closet and come to my mother's rescue.

"That's good, Jonas. Nobody ever needs to know about that."

"Yeah." I exhale loudly. "I mean, it's irrelevant, right? I'm different now. I've conquered myself."

"Oh, yeah. You totally have. You're a badass now, bro. Just look at you. You're a beast."

Emotion is welling up inside me. I suppress it. I pause, considering my words carefully. I need him to understand what Sarah means to me. "Josh, I've told Sarah things I've never told anyone—

not even you." *Because I love her,* I think—but, of course, I don't say it.

"Wow," Josh says. "That's good, Jonas." He gets it. I know he does.

"She understands me." I absentmindedly touch the tattoo on my right forearm. *Visualize the divine originals.* "Sometimes better than I understand myself." I think about Sarah touching this very same spot on my arm and my skin electrifies. "I've never felt like this before," I say softly. *I love her,* I think. *I love her, Josh.* My heart is pounding in my ears.

"Yeah, I can tell." He nods, smiling. "I've never seen you like this about a girl before."

My heart pounds. *Because I love her.*

"So don't fuck it up."

"I won't." God help me, I won't.

Josh exhales loudly and slaps his own face. "Okay, crazy-ass-motherfucker. You know what you gotta do, then?"

I mimic his loud exhale and slap my own face in reply. "Fuck yeah, pussy-ass motherfucker." Slapping ourselves is what Josh and I have always done when we've unexpectedly found ourselves engaged in a conversation about our fucking feelings. It's our mutual way of signaling that it's time to stop acting like crybabies and sack up. I motion to the Club-issued iPhone on the table. "I know exactly what to do."

Josh frowns.

"Hey, I've got to start connecting the dots somehow. I'll start with the only dot I've got. Stacy the Prostitute."

"Jonas . . ."

I scoff. "I'm not gonna *fuck* her, Josh." Even saying those words about Stacy makes my stomach lurch. "Give me some credit."

Josh looks uneasy.

"I'm just gonna check in on the app so I can *talk* to her. I'll butter her up and get her to lead me to her boss. Connect the dots—that's what we said, right?"

Josh grimaces.

"Why do you look like I just gave you a fucking enema? It'll entail nothing but a drink and a quick chat in a crowded bar. Simple."

Josh shakes his head. "Don't kid yourself. It won't be that simple."

"Sure it will. Stacy the Prostitute is just a mercenary—she's chasing the mighty dollar and nothing else. When people are motivated by money, it makes things incredibly simple."

Josh sighs. "But what about Sarah?"

"What about her?"

"She might not think things are as 'simple' as you do."

I stare at him.

"Jonas, think. Sarah might not feel quite so it's-no-big-deal about you meeting up with a woman you've slept with, even if it's just for a 'simple' drink and a chat. Girlfriends are kinda funny that way."

I pause, considering. "Why does she even need to know about it?"

Josh rolls his entire head, not just his eyes. "Oh, for Chrissakes, Jonas, yeah, not telling Sarah would make your fantastic idea even better. Never mind. Forget I ever said a thing about it." Clearly, he's being sarcastic.

"No, really. What's the point in telling her? I'll go meet Stacy at The Pine Box tonight. I'll tell her what she wants to hear—get her to lead me to the next person up the totem pole. Then I come right back home. Done. Simple."

Josh is clearly uneasy. He shakes his head.

"Trust me. Simple."

He exhales. "Just be careful."

"With Stacy?" I laugh. "I'm not afraid of Stacy."

"No, you dumbfuck. I don't mean be careful with *Stacy*." He shakes his head for the hundredth time at me. "I mean be careful with *Sarah*. Don't fuck things up with her. I think you're misjudging this."

I roll my eyes at him. "I'm not."

Why is he worried? This is a great plan. Yes, granted, in a perfect world, Josh's hacker buddy would find these bastards the way he found Sarah for me, and I'd never have to see Stacy again as long as I live. But I can't count on that—Josh himself said so. So I've got to work on Plan B—connecting the dots on my own, one dot at a time, through whatever means necessary.

"Whatcha doin', boys?"

Oh shit. How long has Sarah been standing there?

She's showered and dressed—and, as usual, looking gorgeous.

79

"Hey, baby," I say, quickly closing my laptop. I stand to greet her. "Just plotting world domination." I smile.

She squints at my closed laptop and then at me, her mind instantly whirring and clacking like the well-oiled machine it is.

I embrace her, leaning in to whisper right into her ear. "Last night was incredible, baby. Epic." I kiss her and my entire body starts tingling. She smells delicious.

"The woman wizard strikes again," she whispers, kissing me back. She leans into my ear. "I'm horny as hell this morning, baby— just thinking about last night." Her eyes drift over to Josh and she instantly pulls away from me.

Fucking Josh. I'm glad he's here, of course—I'm the one who called him and asked him to come, I know—but why the fuck is he here?

"Good morning, Sarah Cruz," Josh says politely.

"Good morning, Josh Faraday," Sarah says. She looks at me again. "Thanks for doing my laundry. Wow. You never cease to surprise and delight me, Jonas Faraday." She winks, and I know she's referring to more than her laundry with that compliment.

"You're very, very welcome. It was my supreme pleasure to do your laundry."

"You're exceptionally good at folding clothes, you know that? Impeccable creases."

I smirk. I love it when my baby talks dirty to me.

"If being a business mogul doesn't pan out for you, you could totally work at The Gap."

Josh laughs.

I glare at him. Fuck Josh. Why is he here?

"Did you *iron* my clothes? They're absolutely perfect, like new."

"Of course, I did."

"Babe, that's insane. Are you secretly a housewife from the fifties under there?" She lifts up my T-shirt and peeks at my abs, her knuckles lightly grazing my bare skin as she does. Just this brief touch of her skin on mine gives me goose bumps.

Josh laughs again, making me wonder, yet again, why he's here.

"Excellence in all things," I say softly.

"Absolutely." She smiles at me. She lowers my shirt but doesn't let go of it.

There's a beat. I want her so much it's taking all of my restraint not to clear off my kitchen table. I can't be in this woman's presence for five minutes without wanting to rip her clothes off.

"So," she says, shifting her weight, "besides creating the perfect form of *laundry-ness* in the ideal realm, what else have you been doing with yourself this morning, my sweet Jonas? You've been a busy bee, I presume?" Her eyes drift over to my laptop on the table and unmistakably land with a crashing thud onto my Club-issued iPhone. It's sitting smack in the middle of the table, a fucking beacon of my degeneracy. Fuck. She lets go of my shirt. Her eyes dart back to me. Oh, wow, shit, her eyes are burning like hot coals right now.

"What have you been up to, Jonas?" There's a sudden edge in her voice.

"Just brainstorming a few things with Josh."

"Why'd you close your laptop when I came in?"

I hesitate.

Her eyes dart back to the iPhone again.

"What's that doing there?"

Leave it to Sarah to go straight for the jugular. No fucking around.

I'd really like to lie to her right now, but I can't. Right from day one, I promised her total honesty. I sigh. "I don't want to get you involved with Club stuff. Josh and I are formulating our strategy. We've got it covered."

Josh shoots me a look that unequivocally says, "Leave me the fuck out of it."

Sarah glances back at the kitchen table and glares at the iPhone again.

I shift my weight.

She bites her lip. She looks at Josh. He does his best to remain stone-faced, but he's doing a terrible job of it. She glares at me.

I smile at her reassuringly. Damn, she's adorable when her face is on fire like this.

"Sure thing." Her voice is cool, though her face is hot. "I've got a bunch of stuff to do, anyway."

Her words don't match her body language at all.

"Can I get a ride to my place?" Her eyes drift to my laptop and then again to the iPhone on the table. Her wheels are turning. Her cheeks are red. She's *thinking.* Her eyes are back on me now. "I'm meeting the police at my place in less than an hour. I've got to file a claim about the break-in."

"Whoa, what? Hang on. I'm not sure we should get the police involved. They can't do a damned thing, anyway, and I haven't decided if—"

She cuts me off. "I need to file a police report in order to make a claim on my renter's insurance. I already called my insurance company—I can get a replacement laptop through my policy, I just need to file a police report first."

Oh, she's going to like this. "I already bought you a replacement laptop, baby." I grin broadly and grab it off the nearby counter. My chest is pounding. I've been excited all morning about giving this computer to her. It's loaded with every bell and whistle known to modern technology.

She's quite obviously shocked. "Oh, wow. Thank you." She smiles at me like she pities me. "But no."

I'm not surprised—that's what Kat said at first, too. "Please take the computer," I say. "Help me alleviate my guilty conscience for creating this whole mess in the first place."

She bristles. "You didn't create this mess, Jonas."

"Sarah, don't overthink this. Your computer was stolen. I've got one for you. End of story."

She raises her eyebrows at me.

I probably shouldn't have pushed my luck with that "end of story" caveman shit. "I'm just saying you need a computer and I've got one for you. Simple. Why not?"

"Why not? Because you're far too generous with your money when it comes to me. There's got to be some boundaries, especially if I'm gonna be staying here with you. If you want to take me to a fancy jungle tree house, to a place I could never afford to go on my own, okay, I'm all for it—I want to see the world with you and experience all the things you love to do. Fine. I'll totally take you up on that. Thank you. But you absolutely cannot pay for my basic needs. It's too much. I can't just put my hand out every time I need something. I'm here for *you*, Jonas, not for a hand-out."

God, I hate it when she says shit like that. It reminds me how fucked up she is. Of course, she's not interested in me for my money, that's undeniable. Jesus Christ. I swear to God, she's got the biggest fucking chip on her shoulder when it comes to that. I exhale sharply in frustration. She's not giving me the reaction I expected. Honestly, I was hoping for one of her little squeals. Or, at the very least, a gushing "thank you."

I don't have time or patience for this right now. I just want her to do what I tell her to do for once in her goddamned life. It's time to pull out the trump card.

"Sarah, please. I *insist*." That ought to do the trick.

"Oh, you *insist*, do you?" She laughs. "Well, so do I. I *insist*. So there."

Wait, what? She's not supposed to say that.

Josh makes a noise, suppressing a laugh.

Fuck you, Josh. Why are you here right now?

She kisses me. "Thank you so much, sweet Jonas. You always take such good care of me. But I've got it covered." She looks at her watch. "Oh man, I've got to get to my place to meet the trusty campus police."

"The *campus* police?" Josh laughs. "Oh, I'm sure they'll crack the case in a jiffy."

She laughs. "I know, right? The campus police will protect me from the baddies at The Club, for sure."

Josh and Sarah share a laugh.

Fucking Josh.

"I'll just report a simple break-in and computer theft— obviously, I won't mention The Club. I mean, jeez, I worked for a frickin' brothel." She shakes her head. "I'm not eager to tell anyone that. I'm not even sure I'd pass the ethics review for my legal license if that ever got out." She furrows her brow, genuine concern flashing across her face.

Shit. I hadn't even thought about that. Could this whole thing with The Club torpedo her law career if it ever got out? I'm sure Sarah's freaking out about that. I didn't even consider that angle. I've definitely got to handle this whole situation with kid gloves.

"I'll just let them make a quick report and then I'll have what I need for my insurance claim." The anxiety that flashed across her face a second ago is gone. She's all business now—my little badass. "I've got contracts class right after that, and then I've got to study in

83

the library." She gasps. "Oh, dang it, and I've got to clean up the mess at my place, too—"

"I've arranged a cleaning service to help you with that." She's got to let me do *something* here.

"Oh, Jonas," she sighs. Her entire body melts. She presses her body into mine and moans softly. "You're amazing, you know that? So sweet." She puts her lips right up to my ear. "You just made me wet."

My cock springs to life.

She continues at full voice again. "But my renter's insurance includes a one-time cleaning service, too, for incidents such as this. I already checked." She smiles at me. "So I'm all good."

What the fuck?

"Well . . ." I begin. I'm flustered. I'm turned on. I can't think straight. I'm pissed she's not doing what I want her to do. "I don't think I can return the computer," I babble.

She laughs. "Of course you can. That's just plain silly."

"Maybe not."

"Oh, Jonas." She kisses my neck softly.

My erection is growing. My skin is tingling under her soft lips.

"I guess you'll just have to donate it to a school, then. Or my mom's charity. Or, hey, give it to Trey—I bet he'd be thrilled." Her mouth moves to my lips. "Thank you for being so thoughtful." She kisses me and runs her hand through my hair. She leans into my ear. "Yep, definitely wet."

I'm rock hard.

Why does this woman turn me on like this?

And why does she have to make everything so damned difficult?

She kisses my neck again.

I tilt her face up and kiss her mouth.

Josh gets up from the table and wordlessly leaves the room.

I want her. Now. On the kitchen table. Right now.

She pulls back from me. "So, how about that ride to my place, big boy? I've suddenly figured out the next item on my *addendum*." She smiles wickedly and winks. "Let's see if we can beat the campus fuzz to my place and let them catch us *in flagrante delicto*, shall we?"

Chapter 10
Sarah

I settle into my seat in the big lecture hall. It's about five minutes before the start of my contracts class. And since it's Take Your Boyfriend to Class Day (or so Jonas Faraday has unilaterally decreed), Jonas takes the seat right next to mine. Weird.

I love spending time with Jonas, of course, more than anything, but sitting here in my law school class with him when he should be tending to his brand new chain of indoor rock climbing gyms or acquiring yet another new company or doing whatever mogul-y thing he should be doing right now seems like a waste of his valuable time and resources, not to mention a bizarre case of "two worlds colliding" for me. How long is he planning to put his life on hold to babysit me? It's not realistic. Not to mention slightly awkward. And, frankly, I'm not even convinced it's necessary. I'd never say it to him (because, holy hell, I saw how he reacted when he thought Josh wasn't on board with his Mission to Save Sarah), but I think Jonas might be overreacting just a teensy-weensy bit here.

I was shocked and scared and freaking out yesterday when we first discovered the break-in at my apartment, and, yes, I lost my mind with worry when we found out Kat's apartment had suffered the same fate as mine, but after the initial shock wore off, I got to thinking about the situation, and I'm not sure The Club poses a genuine threat to me, at least not a physical one. If these guys were violent criminals, then why'd they even bother breaking into my apartment? It would have made a lot more sense to lie in wait for me and take care of things more definitively. My hunch is they were merely gathering information by taking my computer and then decided to trash the place as an afterthought. They're just cyber-pimps, after all. Who's ever heard of a violent cyber-pimp?

I've definitely got to tell Jonas what I think about all this. But this morning just didn't seem like the time to do it—especially after the way he reacted to Josh last night. I figure I'll tackle that issue with him tomorrow—ever so gently—and, in the meantime, I'll just tackle *him.* Whenever I get the chance, that is, because this morning certainly didn't work out as planned.

My big idea this morning was to lure Jonas into "oh no, maybe someone will see us!" sex at my apartment—a safe and seemingly easy way to invoke the spectator-hotness from last night's sizzling dream. I planned to attack Jonas at my place before the campus police arrived, leaving the front door open a crack for Campus Johnny Law to enter. I imagined Jonas and me going at it, hot and heavy in my ransacked bedroom, maybe even with my bedroom door slightly ajar, both of us on the verge of pure ecstasy, until we—gasp!—heard the men in blue stomping around my living room. I imagined the police calling out to me from the other side of my bedroom wall, perhaps concerned for my safety, given the disarray of my apartment.

"Miss Cruz?" they'd say. "It's the police!"

At which point Jonas and I would jolt apart, just in time to avoid being caught by the fuzz with our pants down (literally). The whole idea gets me going like crazy, just thinking about it.

Unfortunately, though, my "Oh no, maybe someone will see us!" fantasy just wasn't in the cards. When Jonas and I arrived at my apartment, the trusty campus police were already waiting inside—the superintendent had let them in, worried something had happened to me—and by the time the police left (after having written out a quick and meaningless report, as predicted), it was time to hightail it over to my contracts class.

I look at my watch. We've still got a few minutes before class starts.

Jonas places the laptop he bought for me on my desktop. He's had it with him in a small carrying case since we left his house, but I thought he'd brought it with him so he could return it.

"This is yours," Jonas says, his voice soft but commanding. "I got it for you because I want to take care of you in every conceivable way."

Before I can respond, he continues.

"If and when you get a replacement laptop through your insurance, you can give that one to your mom or donate it to a school or do whatever the fuck you want with it. But this one is yours, and only yours, Sarah, because *I* got it for you."

He looks exactly like he did when he tied those matching friendship bracelets around our wrists in Belize. I can't help but look down at the multi-colored bracelet around my wrist and then at its match on Jonas' wrist. And just like that, my heart melts like an ice cube on a hot skillet.

"Thank you," I say softly, leaning over to kiss him.

His relief is palpable as he greets my lips with his own.

When his tongue enters my mouth, my body bursts into flames. And when he brings his hands to my face and caresses my cheeks with his thumbs, my heart races and my breathing halts. I'm blazing hot right now, not surprisingly—I've been sexed up like a banshee all morning long, sense memories of last night's intimate festivities (especially my unexpected transformation into Orgasma the All-Powerful) floating through my head (and several other parts of my anatomy, too). Holy hot dam, I'm on fire, ready to go off at the slightest touch.

"Miss Cruz?" My professor's voice rings out into the large lecture hall.

I jerk away from Jonas and wipe my mouth with the back of my hand. Every eyeball in the entire class, including my professor's, is trained on me. I can feel my cheeks blazing crimson.

"Who's our guest?" my professor asks, not a trace of amusement on her face.

"I'm sorry, Professor Martin. This is Jonas," I say. "He's going to sit in on class today, if that's okay with you."

"Well, hello there, *Jonas*," my professor says, her voice softening as she takes in the glorious sight of him—she is a woman, after all. "You have a deep and abiding interest in contracts, I take it?"

I'm expecting Jonas to be mortified by Professor Martin's attention, but he surprises me by being smooth as silk.

"As a matter of fact, I do," he replies. "I'd be grateful if you'd allow me to sit in today."

"All right," my professor says, her entire demeanor warming and melting before my eyes. "We go by last names here," she says. "What shall we call you, sir?'

"Mr. Faraday," he responds, charisma oozing out his pores.

Instant recognition flashes in her eyes. "Jonas Faraday—of Faraday & Sons?"

Jonas nods. "That's right."

"What a nice surprise for us, Mr. Faraday. Welcome."

"Thank you."

"You could *teach* this class, I'm sure. You've negotiated a contract or two in your lifetime, yes?"

Jonas smiles and his eyes twinkle at her. "Maybe once or twice."

She addresses the entire lecture hall, her face suddenly beaming. "If Mr. Faraday is willing, this would be an excellent opportunity for you to learn about how contracts work in the real world." She directs her stare at Jonas again, smiling. "Would you be so kind as to answer a few questions for us today, Mr. Faraday?"

"I'll do my best, Professor."

Professor Martin laughs—something I've rarely seen the woman do.

"Wonderful," she says, bubbling over with enthusiasm. "Why don't you come on up here with me?" She pats a stool up front.

Oh boy, it's on like Donkey Kong. I can feel it. Jonas saunters to the front of the room, his butt a glorious sight in his jeans, his T-shirt clinging to his broad shoulders and muscled back, and I can feel half the class, men and women alike, swooning. When he takes his offered seat at the front of the class and smiles, his biceps bulging out of his short sleeves, the other half of the class falls under his spell, too.

For the next hour, Jonas elegantly and artfully, and with mesmerizing confidence, answers every question the professor and students ask. With the most adorable twinkle in his eye, and the most thoughtful tilt of his head, and an occasional, sensual lick of those luscious lips, he tells us about how contracts work in the world of complex business transactions—how they're formed, negotiated, and what really happens as a practical matter when they're breached (as opposed to what our textbooks say happens). He tells us what role his own lawyers play when advising him regarding multimillion-dollar deals, and, most humorously, why he so often chooses to ignore his lawyers' "impractical and deal-killing" advice and forge ahead, anyway.

"As an entrepreneur, I'm all about stepping on the proverbial gas pedal with a lead foot—getting the deal done. The lawyers, on the other hand, or, as I most often call them, the *effing* lawyers—except I don't say 'effing'" —everyone in the classroom laughs, even Professor Martin, and so do I—though I'm laughing because it's the first time I've heard Jonas use "effing" in place of his favorite word and it sounds comical coming out of his mouth—"tend to perceive their job as convincing me that a sane and prudent person would slam on the brakes. The thing is, in business, sanity and prudence are vastly overrated. The business world rewards risk-takers—the bigger the risk, the bigger the reward."

It's objectively the most interesting and thought-provoking contracts class we've ever had. And the sexiest. The man is gorgeous. Irresistible. Magnetic. Masculine. Brilliant. He's got the entire classroom in the palm of his magical hand. Every woman around me is swooning over this beautiful man—I'm pretty sure I can hear eggs spontaneously popping out of ovaries all around me. Even my professor can't keep her inner fangirl from coming out.

"Such an interesting perspective, Mr. Faraday," Professor Martin gushes when time runs out. "And so well articulated. Thank you so much for joining us. What a lucky surprise." She glances at me when she says the word "lucky" and I blush.

It occurs to me that if Jonas were to ask Professor Martin to come home with him tonight and spread her creamy thighs on his crisp white sheets, she'd say yes. Or, more accurately, "oh, hell yes—let's go right now."

"Come back and join us any time," my professor coos to Jonas in the last moments of class.

"Thank you for your hospitality, Professor," Jonas says, flashing his most outrageously charming smile.

As Jonas walks back up the aisle toward me, everyone applauds in appreciation—and quite a few of them also steal envious glances at me, too.

Why her?

What makes her so special?

I can't believe she gets to have sex with a man who looks like that.

It's as though I can hear their thoughts bouncing off the walls.

89

He's mine, I send back to them. *Mine, mine, mine, mine, mine.* It's all I can do not to re-enact last night's dream right here, right now, in front of all of them, right on top of Professor Martin's desktop.

"You were magnificent," I tell Jonas when he reaches me at my desk. "So knowledgeable. Confident yet self-deprecating." I smile broadly at him. "Ridiculously charming."

"Thanks. I hated every minute of it." He takes the seat next to me.

"No, you didn't. You *think* you did, but you didn't."

He rolls his eyes. "Is this the part where you tell me what I *think* I want isn't actually what I want?"

"You were in your element. You can't fake something like that. You were brilliant."

"I would rather have been sitting here next to you." His eyes are earnest.

Damn, those eyes of his. They get me every time.

"Let's go to the library," I whisper. "I've got something I need to do."

"Sure," Jonas replies. But then he catches something in my expression that makes him smile broadly at me. "Whatever you say, baby—I'm all yours."

Chapter 11
Sarah

"Tell me about your dream," Jonas says softly. "The one that made you come in your sleep."

We're standing in the massive law library, deep in the bowels of the book stacks. He's got me pinned against a metal bookshelf stacked floor-to-ceiling with thick legal tomes.

He kisses my neck. "Tell me all about it, pretty baby." His erection bulges inside his jeans. He glides his hand up my thigh, underneath my skirt, and onto my bare ass cheek. He lets out a soft moan as his hand gropes me and pulls me into him. "I love this ass."

I'm trembling with my desire for him.

He nips at my ear. "Tell me what turned you on so much that you came in your sleep."

"I'm such a big girl now, aren't I? Coming all by myself like that."

"You *are* a big girl. A beautiful, sexy, irresistible girl."

His hand moves to the cotton crotch of my G-string and caresses me lightly. I lift my leg up and around him, inviting him inside me. His fingers push the pesky fabric of my panties aside and brush lightly across my sensitive flesh.

I shudder.

He brushes his fingers lightly across me again, and when my pelvis thrusts involuntarily toward him in response, his fingers dip ever so gently into my wetness.

I moan softly.

"You like that?"

"Mmm hmm."

I like that a whole lot, thank you, and a few other things, too. For instance, I also like the way every woman in that classroom looked at Jonas like they wanted to fuck him. And I like that they can't have him because he's all mine. And I like how, right before we left the classroom, he cupped my face in his hands and kissed me softly in front of all those staring eyes and then grabbed my hand and brought my thumb ring to his warm lips.

Just behind me in the next aisle over, two students walk by. They're chatting softly as they go. I turn my head and peek at them through the cracks between books. They keep walking past, oblivious to the well-hung cowboy and his horny little pony groping each other just a few feet away on the other side of the bookshelf.

Jonas' fingers continue working their magic on me. A loud moan threatens to escape my throat, so I bite his neck.

"Ow," Jonas says in surprise. "Jesus. Why so violent?"

I stifle my giggle.

Movement flickers in the spaces between the books and someone coughs behind us. We both freeze, grinning at each other like kids removing the lid off a cookie jar.

Whoever it is, they keep moving down the aisle.

"Come on, My Magnificent Sarah." His fingers resume their exploration. "Tell me what turned you on so much."

I unbutton his jeans.

"It was the most erotic dream I've ever had," I whisper.

"I like that word."

"Erotic?"

He nods.

"Erotic... erotic... erotic." Each word is accompanied by a wet kiss on his neck. "*Un sueño erótico.*"

He moans softly. Jonas loves it when I speak Spanish.

I lick his neck where I bit him a moment ago.

"Tell me."

I tell him about my dream and why it was so deliriously arousing to me—at least, I try to tell him. Talking is surprisingly hard to do when there are magic fingers massaging your wahoo and soft lips kissing your skin and warm breath in your ear.

When I'm done talking, it's quite obvious he's turned on by my dream, too.

"The red wine was dripping all over your skin?"

"Mmm hmm."

"Over your clit?" His voice has turned husky.

"Mmm."

"And I was licking it up?" He exhales a soft groan.

"You were everywhere all at once."

"Licking you?" Oh yeah, he's really turned on.

"Fucking me, kissing me, touching me, licking me, eating me. All at once."

He grips my ass and pulls me into him. "Sounds like heaven." His lips skim mine as his fingers move in and out of me.

I'm panting. "But it was still *you*. Every mouth and penis and finger was *yours*. That's why it turned me on." I don't want him to misunderstand and think I'm craving some sort of orgy, because I'm not. Even in my dreams, I only want him—one at a time, ten at a time, like a poltergeist, whatever, it doesn't matter, as long as it's him. I only want him. *Jonas Faraday.*

My hand moves into his jeans. He exhales when my fingers find his erection. It's enormous, ready for business. I yank down on the waistband of his briefs and peel back the front of his jeans, freeing his hard-on. He groans as his erection springs out of his pants.

"You're a human Jack in the Box."

He grins. "Only if you're the box."

I bite his shoulder, stifling my laughter.

He nips at my ear. "Back to your dream, baby." His fingers continue manipulating me with astonishing precision. "The people watching—that turned you on?"

"Mmm." I can't say anything more than that. His fingers have found the exact spot that makes me crazy. It's all I can do not to scream right here in the library. My body has begun jerking and grinding like crazy. I'm on fire. "Oh, God, Jonas," I murmur, my pleasure rising. "Yes."

A young woman enters our row, down at the end, headed toward us. We both briefly freeze. She stops dead in her tracks, a stricken look on her face, and quickly strides away in the opposite direction.

We both burst out laughing. I bury my mouth into his broad shoulder again, trying to silence myself.

"We've scarred her for life," Jonas whispers.

"Sucks to be her."

Jonas' fingers resume what they were doing. His fingers slide from my wetness to my tip and back again, over and over. I shudder.

"You like that?"

I nod enthusiastically. "Mmm."

"You like the idea of people watching us fuck?" he clarifies.

Oh, I thought he was asking me about his magic fingers. "Mmm hmm." My hand moves up and down his shaft. His tip is already wet—he's ready to blow. I'm so turned on, I can barely stand.

He lets out a soft moan. "Why?" He exhales. He kisses my lips and the pleasure zings me right between my legs—it's as if a live wire runs directly from my lips to my clit. His free hand grazes my back and unfastens my bra from underneath my T-shirt. He pulls my shirt up and licks my breast. His tongue swirls around my nipple. My clit flutters violently.

I moan. I can't take it anymore. "Now," I whisper.

He ignores me, as usual. He lowers my shirt and grabs my ass under my skirt again.

I grind myself into him. "Now," I say again.

"Why did you like people watching us?"

I raise my leg even higher around him and tilt myself toward him. "Come on, Jonas, right now."

"Patience, baby." He sucks on my lower lip and my entire body convulses. "You never learn, do you?"

I shake my head. It's true. I never learn.

"First tell me why you liked being watched. Tell me why and I'll fuck you."

I'm almost desperate now. I'm tempted to kneel and take him into my mouth—I want him inside me, any way I can get him—but I resist the urge. We are in a library, after all. "Because they all wanted you. Every single one of them wanted you." I stroke him vigorously.

He makes a primal sound and shudders. He yanks on my G-string under my skirt and pulls it down roughly, making me moan in anticipation.

His fingers are spellbinding. Oh my God, he's so talented. I can't stand it anymore. "No more prelude, Jonas," I whisper. "Do it now."

He spreads my legs slightly with his thigh, making me shudder, and shifts his body into position to enter into me. "Who cares if they want me?" He grabs my ass with both hands and lifts me up, pinning me against the bookshelf. "Tell me why it turned you on and I'll fuck you."

He wedges himself between my legs, his tip rubbing deliciously against my clit.

I throw my head back against the bookshelf, bracing myself for him. I want him inside me. I'm shaking. I'm panting.

"Why do you care if anyone else wants me? All that matters is you want me."

He's teasing me wickedly. I'm throbbing, licking my lips, aching. My pelvis is thrusting involuntarily in anticipation of him. "Fuck me right now. Oh my God, Jonas."

"Tell me first."

I groan. "They all wanted you, but they couldn't have you. I liked showing them you're mine. *You're all mine, Jonas.*" I whimper. "*Mine.*"

He suddenly withdraws from me and straightens up.

"What the fuck?" he whispers. He stuffs himself quickly back into his jeans.

My cheeks instantly flush with shame.

Oh my God. I thought he'd *like* hearing me say he's all mine. I open my mouth, a confused apology on the tip of my tongue, but then I quickly see that, no, that's not it, he's not reacting to what I said—he's peering through the spaces between the books opposite him, his eyes narrowed to menacing slits. I peek behind me and stare in the direction of his sightline, but I don't see anything.

He whips his head and glares at me, suddenly full of intensity. He grabs my shoulders forcefully. "Stay right here. Don't move from this spot." Without another word, he races down the aisle, fastening his jeans as he goes. At the end of the bookshelf, he makes a sharp right turn and vanishes into the stacks of books.

My mouth hangs open—along with my legs, my bra, my panties, my shirt, and my ego. Not to mention my vajayjay. What just happened? I quickly put myself back together. I'm trembling. What the hell? I wait for him to come back for a good two minutes—okay, maybe for a minute and a half. Okay, fine, for a solid minute. Or so. Maybe less. I've got to figure out what's going on.

I walk slowly toward the end of the aisle, to the spot where

Jonas turned the corner and disappeared, my heart pounding in my ears. When I get to the end of the bookshelf, I peek around it, afraid of what I might find. But there's only a couple of students chatting quietly in another aisle. No Jonas. I creep slowly in the same direction Jonas went, my chest tight and breathing shaky.

His eyes were wild when he told me to stay put. He didn't even look like himself for a minute there. He looked like a man possessed. Like a lunatic.

Still no Jonas.

I creep to the perimeter of the maze, goose bumps covering my entire body. Where is he? I keep walking until I reach a small window overlooking the parking lot. I peek out. I can make out his BMW in a distant corner of the lot. That's a good sign—at least I know he's still here somewhere.

A hand grabs my shoulder.

I gasp.

"I told you not to move, Sarah." He's angry. His eyes have that wild look in them again.

"I... What happened?"

"I need to get you out of here. I'm taking you home."

"What happened? What did you see?"

"If I tell you not to move, then don't fucking move, you understand? From now on, you listen to me. This isn't a game."

"What's going on?"

His eyes blaze with sudden intensity. "When we were in the lecture hall, when I was sitting up front, this palooka-looking guy came in the back door and stood there for a couple minutes. He looked like fucking John Travolta in *Pulp Fiction* or something, like he was wearing a two-bit-hoodlum costume for Halloween. Total cliché."

I shrug. I don't understand what that has to do with anything.

He exhales. "He didn't look like a law student."

I still don't understand. I'm sure there are plenty of two-bit-thuggy-looking people milling around any college campus anywhere in the United States at any given time—students, boyfriends of students, fathers of students, janitors, vending machine repairmen, stalkers, rapists, murderers, creepers. I mean, aren't there weirdos and freaks and criminals and people who *look* like weirdos and freaks and criminals at any given place at any given time—especially on college campuses—none of them affiliated in any way with The Club?

"Jonas . . ." I begin.

"I thought he was staring at you in the classroom, but I couldn't be sure—I thought maybe I was imagining things." His eyes are fierce.

I wait.

"But I just saw that same fucker again—right over there—" He motions into the stacks. "And this time I'm absolutely positive he was watching us—one hundred percent sure."

The hairs on the back of my neck stand up.

"When I spotted him, he took off running." He clenches his fists. "Fuck."

"Maybe he was just a student? Or a voyeur?"

He runs his hand through his hair. "Is there a student in your contracts class—or in the entire law school—who looks like a hitman from a Quentin Tarantino movie?"

I shake my head. "Not that I've seen. Bill Gates and Ashton Kutcher doppelgangers, yes. Dancing heroin addicts with ponytails, not so much." I'm trying to make him smile, but it's not working at all.

His jaw muscle pulses. His eyes are steel. "This isn't a joke, Sarah." He's pissed at me.

"I know."

His eyes flicker with something animalistic—he's kinda scary right now, actually.

I sigh.

I can't decide if my sweet Jonas is being overly protective of me (or, worse, maybe even a touch paranoid), or if the bad guys truly are gunning for me as vigorously as he thinks they are. That'd be pretty ballsy, wouldn't it, for the bad guys to waltz right into my classroom in broad daylight?

"You're sure it was the same guy in both places?"

He exhales with exasperation. "I'm absolutely fucking positive. Why the fuck are you doubting me on this?" His jaw is clenched.

"I . . ." I can't finish the sentence. He's right—I'm doubting him. Why? Are my lifelong trust issues rearing their ugly head again? I don't think so. Am I in deep denial about the situation, ignoring real danger as a means of emotional self-preservation? Highly doubtful. Or could it be that I secretly think my gorgeous hunk of a boyfriend is just a wee bit crazy (not that there's anything wrong with that)—that his judgment might be a teensy bit impaired in situations such this (understandably), due to the horrific trauma of his past? I bite my lip. Yup. I'm pretty sure it's Door Number Three. Damn.

I look into his eyes. Oh God, he's got beautiful eyes. And he's looking at me like I'm a rare treasure—the Mona Lisa—and he's just recovered me from the clutches of a master art thief. He pulls me into him and squeezes me tight.

"If I tell you to stay put, then stay put."

I return his embrace. "Okay."

Suddenly, a non sequitur of a thought slams me upside the head and punches me in the gut: *What was your Club-issued iPhone doing out on the kitchen table this morning, Jonas?* Why that seemingly random thought crashes into my brain at this particular moment, I have no idea, but, clearly, my subconscious brain sees some connection between that goddamned iPhone and my reticence to unconditionally adopt his belief in my imminent demise.

He buries his face in my hair and breathes in my scent.

"Don't ever scare me like that again, Sarah." He leans down and kisses me gently. "Come on. I'm getting you the fuck out of here."

Chapter 12
Jonas

I look at my watch. Quarter to seven. Stacy the Faker should be here in fifteen minutes.

"A Heineken," I tell the bartender. He nods his acknowledgment.

I look around the bar.

I hope Stacy doesn't call me out for not wearing that stupid purple bracelet. I know I'm technically required to wear it at all times during Club check-ins, but I threw it into the trash the minute Stacy left my house after our horrible fuck. And, anyway, even if I still had it, there's no way I'd put that thing on my wrist. Now that every part of me, including my wrist, belongs to Sarah, that piece-of-shit purple bracelet would probably sear my flesh like a hot iron brand.

I touch the multi-colored yarn bracelet on my wrist, one-half of the pair I got in Belize for Sarah and me. My mind drifts to the moment I tied Sarah's matching bracelet onto her wrist. The look on her face was so beautiful at that moment, so honest and vulnerable—so pure. I think that's when I knew I loved her for sure—when I tied that bracelet on her and told her she's my perfect match and she looked like she was going to cry.

No, wait, it was before then that I knew I loved her—what am I thinking? *Of course.* It was when she leaped off that waterfall into the dark abyss below. She was scared shitless, but she did it anyway, because she knew I was down there waiting for her in the dark water, waiting to catch her, and that I'd never let any harm come to her. She did it because she was finally ready to take a leap of faith with me— well, that and I'd left her no other way down. I smile at that last part. She wasn't even mad at me for luring her up there with no other option—she understood my intentions. She always understands. And so she rose to the occasion, like she always does—and just let go and trusted me and trusted herself and jumped into the void.

Yeah, definitely, that's the moment I knew—when she plunged into the cold, dark water and threw her arms around my neck, shivering and shaking with fear and adrenaline and elation, and wouldn't let go of me. She clutched me like her very life depended on me, like I was her life raft. And that's when I knew I couldn't live without her because I clutched her right back, just has tightly, just as desperately, if not more so. And every moment since then, I've been clutching her more and more fiercely, becoming more and more sure of my feelings for her—more and more certain she's my life raft, too. I've never been so sure of anything in my entire life, in fact.

The bartender puts my beer in front of me.

I throw down a ten and take a big gulp.

Thank God I didn't throw my Club iPhone away along with that stupid purple bracelet. I was this close to tossing it, actually, but then it hit me I might be able to wipe the damned thing completely clean and give it to Trey—it's a perfectly good iPhone, after all. So I threw it into a drawer in my kitchen, intending to deal with it later, and promptly forgot all about it—until this morning, that is, when I was brainstorming for my "How I'm Going to Fuck The Club Up the Ass" spreadsheet.

As it turned out, it was a huge stroke of luck I'd kept that phone, or else right now I'd have no fucking idea how to begin connecting the dots within The Club to a power player. Josh's hacker already called right before I left for the bar, saying the emails Josh and I forwarded to him are all dead ends, every single one of them, completely untraceable. Josh wasn't surprised at all and took it in stride, but I was deflated. It meant I had to go through with meeting Stacy here tonight. What other option do I have? She's my only lead. I've got to do whatever I can to track these fuckers down and keep Sarah safe.

I take another swig of my beer and look around.

There are some really good-looking people here tonight. But, then again, there are always good-looking people at The Pine Box. That's why this used to be one of my favorite hunting grounds—well, that, and it's within walking distance of my place. That sure used to make things easy. No worrying about whose car we'd take back to my place—we only ever had hers, which also conveniently meant she could easily leave my place in the morning without a messy hassle. Shit, those days of fucking a different woman virtually every night seem like a lifetime ago. I don't even feel like the same guy. Sarah's changed everything in such a short amount of time, just like I knew she would. Just like I hoped she would.

Another long swig of my beer. Fuck it. I chug the rest. I flag down the bartender and hold up my empty bottle. He nods. My knee jiggles wildly. I force it to stop.

A brunette with a pixie cut and large hoop earrings smiles at me from the corner. I look away. The old me would have gone over to her. She's hot. Pretty face. And her whole look screams confidence, a trait that always attracts me. But I don't give a shit. All I can think about is Sarah. She's all I want. I can't wait to get out of here and go back home to her.

Sarah didn't bat an eyelash when I told her I had to slip away for a bit, that I had something I had to do.

"No problem, baby," she said. "I've got a ton of studying to do."

She's so diligent about her studies, so determined to get that scholarship at the end of the year. I love that about her. She sees what she wants and goes after it, relentlessly.

"I won't be gone long," I assured her. "I'll come back as soon as I can."

"Take your time. God knows you can't sit here babysitting me for the rest of your life. I'll be here," she said. "I've got so much to do."

I've never met a woman with such a slender jealous streak. She just trusts me. My stomach suddenly churns at the thought—yeah, Sarah trusts me, and I'm *here*, waiting for Stacy.

"I won't be gone long," I said again. "And Josh will be here the whole time to look after you."

"Okeedoke." She already had her nose buried in a book.

"Promise me you'll stay here and not go anywhere."

She rolled her eyes and looked up from her book. "Jonas, don't act like a weirdo. I've got to study, I told you. I'm so effing behind it's ridiculous. Trust me, I'm not going anywhere."

"But promise me, Sarah. Say, 'I promise, Jonas.'"

"Jeez," she said, scrunching up her nose. "That's not creepy or anything." At my insistent expression, she rolled her eyes again. "Okay, Lord-God-Master, I promise." She flashed me a smart-ass smirk. "You always say I'm bossy, but I think that's the pot calling the kettle bossy."

When my expression remained anxious, she laughed.

"I'll be right here, Jonas. Just go do whatever you've got to do, Mr. Mogul. Thanks to you and your red hot lovin' day and night, I'm woefully behind in my reading for criminal law and torts. I'm gonna study all night long without a single break."

"Well, hang on a second," I replied, forcing her book closed and pulling her into me. "I don't want you studying *all* night long. You're gonna have to take a break at some point for more of my red hot lovin'."

"Well, hmm," she said. "If you *insist.*" She laughed and kissed me. "Duh, Jonas. Making love to you every single night is a given. It's a physical necessity—right up there with breathing and eating and peeing."

I smile to myself. *My Magnificent Sarah.*

I check my watch. Seven o'clock on the button. Any minute now. The hairs on my arms stand at attention at the thought of seeing Stacy again. My knee jiggles again. I can't make it stop. My stomach flip-flops. I banged Stacy so sloppily—and she acted like she was in the throes of pure ecstasy the whole time. The whole thing was just revolting. And then to think she cornered Sarah in the bathroom at that sports bar and threatened her? Okay, I have to stop thinking about all the ways Stacy disgusts me—I've got to put myself in the right frame of mind to charm her.

And there she is. Right on cue, strutting into the bar in a little black dress and sky-high heels. I raise my arm and flag her down. She nods and smiles broadly at me, and even from this distance, I can plainly see the purple bracelet on her wrist. The sight of it makes me recoil, but I force myself to smile.

"Well, hello again," she says, approaching the bar. "*Jonas.*"

"Hi, Stacy." I put my hand out to shake just as she leans in for a hug. It's momentarily awkward. I play it off like I'm just a shy dork and quickly lean in to give her a brief hug. Yeah, I guess it's kind of weird to shake hands with someone you've already fucked, huh? I need to get my head in the game and act like I'm happy to see her.

"Chardonnay?"

"You remember. Yes, I'd love it. Thanks."

I order her drink.

Sarah.

This is totally fucked up what I'm doing right now. It feels wrong. I just have to remember why I'm doing it. I'll have a quick drink with Stacy, that's all—with this woman who happens to be a prostitute—a prostitute I've fucked—and get the information I need. And then I'll race home and lick my baby's sweet pussy with extra zeal and make her come, maybe even over and over, if I'm lucky.

"Let's sit at a table," I suggest.

"How about that one over there?"

Stacy points to a booth in the corner—the one where Sarah and Kat spied on me when I first met Stacy. I can see the ghost of Menu Girl sitting there right now, her forearms and hands taunting me with their olive-toned smoothness, her long dark hair cascading around her shoulders from behind her menu. I hadn't even laid eyes on Sarah yet, hadn't even seen a photo of her, but my soul already knew she owned me, even then.

Stacy's eyes are bullets.

Is she trying to communicate something to me by suggesting that particular booth? Is this some kind of a test?

"No, not that one," I say. My eyes are steely. I know they are. I've got to grab ahold of myself and try to channel Charming Jonas right now. Supreme Dick Extraordinaire Jonas isn't going to get the job done. "Over here." I lead her to another booth at the opposite end of the bar and we sit.

Stacy takes a sip of her wine and eyeballs me. "So nice to hear from you again, Jonas. I'm glad you requested me. I was hoping you would."

I nod. "The pleasure's all mine. Thank you for agreeing to see me again."

"Of course. I had a great time with you that first time. I was hoping you'd want an encore."

There's a beat.

I sigh. "Let's talk turkey, shall we?"

She raises her eyebrows.

"I had a little fling with my intake agent—the woman who reviewed my application."

"Oh," Stacy says, seemingly having a genuine epiphany. "*That's who she was?*"

Stacy must be extremely low on the totem pole if she didn't know Sarah's identity until now.

I lean in like I'm telling her a secret. "I'm a bit of an adrenaline junkie. I couldn't help myself—forbidden fruit and all that."

She smiles. Charming Jonas has definitely come out tonight.

"Which one was it? The blonde or the brunette?"

"The brunette. It's always brunettes for me."

Stacy's eyes sparkle. Brunettes always love to hear a man say he prefers brunettes to blondes.

"And brunettes with blue eyes are my absolute favorite."

I'm laying it on a bit thick, I know, but shit, I don't have all day. I want to get the fuck out of here so I can go home to my beautiful brown-eyed girl.

"Who was the blonde, then? Another intake agent?"

"No, just the intake agent's friend. The blonde doesn't know anything about The Club—to this day, she thinks she was spying on some guy her friend met on Match.com." Hopefully, that little tidbit of information will find its way up the totem pole and clear Kat from their crosshairs.

Stacy laughs. "Oh, that's hilarious. I thought . . ." She stops, unsure of how much I know. Obviously, she doesn't want to unwittingly step into a steaming pile of shit.

"You thought they were new girls, poaching on your territory?"

Stacy raises her eyebrows and twists her mouth in acknowledgment.

"Yeah, so I heard. That's why I wanted to see you, actually."

Stacy's eyes narrow. "Oh yeah? Why's that?"

"Well, I'm not gonna lie—I had a really nice time with my intake agent. She was a lot of fun. But it's over now. She got all clingy—you know how that is. I can't stand clingy."

"Oh God, neither can I."

"Well, see, that's what I figured—because you're a pro, Stacy. And I like that."

Her eyes ripple with surprise.

I take a long sip of my beer, eying her. "My intake agent told me all about her encounter with you at that sports bar, when you were wearing the yellow bracelet with that other guy." Stacy reflexively looks down at the purple bracelet on her wrist, like she's trying to remember which color she's wearing tonight. "And I gotta tell you—it really turned me on."

Stacy's face reflects earnest surprise. "It did? What about that turned you on?"

"Are you kidding me? You're not emotionally invested. You staked out your territory—told her not to fuck with you. You're here to do a job and do it well. I respect that. Like I said, you're a total pro. A badass."

She blushes at the compliment. She's buying what I'm selling. "Thank you." She tilts her head and smiles. "So you like a badass kind of girl, huh?" She reaches across the table and strokes the top of my hand.

I instinctively jerk my hand away. The woman makes my flesh crawl. I play it off like I'm reaching for my beer.

"Frankly," I continue, swigging my beer again, "I was relieved to find out the real deal about The Club. Elated, even. The whole reason I joined in the first place was to avoid emotional attachments, you know? Women always get so... *emotional.* It really ruins the fun for me. That's what happened with the intake agent, too. She was a sweetheart, a great girl, but then she got emotionally attached, just couldn't distinguish sex from some sort of fairytale fantasy."

"Sounds like you need a pro." She winks.

"Exactly. Someone I can just be totally *honest* with, you know?"

Stacy raises one eyebrow suggestively. "What would you like to be honest about, Jonas?"

I finish off my beer and flash her my most dazzling smile. "About what each of us wants—what we *really* want."

She leans forward, ready to hear it.

"You're in it for the money." I smile. "And that's good. And I'm in it for the sex. Period. I just want to fuck a beautiful woman, whenever I feel like it, no strings attached. None of the bullshit."

One side of her mouth hitches up. "Well, that sounds good to me." She stands. "Let's get the hell out of here, shall we?"

Oh shit. "Hang on a minute. My idea is a bit bigger than that—bigger than just tonight. Sit down and let me tell you what I have in mind."

She sits back down. "I'm all ears." She licks her lips.

My stomach somersaults. I'm having a flashback of my tongue on her cunt.

"First off, let me just tell you how incredible you are in bed." I'm using the word incredible in its literal sense—*not credible*.

She bats her eyelashes. "It was my pleasure. You were amazing."

"Aw, that's sweet," I say, making myself smile. That's the phrase Sarah uses when she's actually calling me a dumbass. *Aw, that's sweet, Jonas,* she always says, her eyes laughing at me. "But you were the incredible one, Stacy." I feel like I'm going to hurl. "The way you came so fast and so hard? That was just... *incredible.*"

"It was all you."

"I really like it when women come—have you read my application?"

She shrugs. "It's been a little while—remind me." She flashes her most seductive smile.

Yeah, I'm sure she's read more than a few applications since mine. "I really get off on making women come—especially since it's so hard to do. I like the challenge of it. Sometimes it takes me a whole month to figure out how to do it with a particular woman." I chuckle. "Women are complicated."

She laughs and nods. "We sure are."

"But I usually manage it somehow, after lots of practice. Not always, of course, but, usually. But with you, it was right away— boom—and so intense, too. That was just totally *incredible,* Stacy. I haven't stopped thinking about it since."

Stacy smiles. "Yeah. It was awesome."

"So I've been seeing my intake agent lately, like I said, and she's just not like you, Stacy, not at all. One hundred eighty degrees different. She doesn't get off the way you did—not at all—and, lately, I just can't stop thinking about how much I want to be with a woman who embraces her own desires, who knows what she wants— a woman who can let go and surrender to her pleasure without holding back." In other words, I want my Sarah.

Stacy beams at me. "Sounds good to me," she says. "Why don't we start right now?" Clearly, she's politely trying to move this party along. Maybe she's hoping to squeeze in another check-in later tonight if I'd just hurry the fuck up.

"Hang on. I have a proposition for you."

She tilts her head to the side, ready for whatever I'm going to say.

"I'd like to purchase a block of your time."

"Oh." She smiles. "What do you have in mind?"

"Two weeks."

Her smile widens. "You want a GFE."

"What's that?"

"A Girlfriend Experience."

I can't keep my lip from curling. The only GFE I want is with Sarah.

"Right," I force myself to say. "GFE. I'll pay extra, of course—over and above what I've already paid to The Club for my membership. I think that's fair because I want you exclusively. I don't want to wear my purple bracelet, worry about check-ins, etcetera. I just want to take you out of the Club rotation for a couple weeks and have you all to myself. I'd be willing to pay The Club a premium for the privilege—let's say the equivalent of a month's membership?"

"How much is a month's membership?"

"You don't know?"

"No. I get paid per job."

"How much do you get paid per job?"

She pauses. "Five hundred."

She's full of shit. She just doubled her real take. Clever girl. But whatever. Even using Stacy's bullshit number, I quickly do the math in my head. Even if a member checks in every day for thirty days, even after The Club pays their intake agents and whatever other overhead, whoever's running this shit show must clear close to fifteen thousand per month, per member—and they must have thousands, if not tens of thousands, of members. Oh my God, they're making money hand over fist.

"Monthly membership costs thirty thousand."

Stacy's eyes sparkle, though she tries to act like that number doesn't impress her.

"Maybe I could negotiate a deal with your boss to get you a bigger piece of the pie than usual? I could sit down with him and—"

"With *her*."

My heart leaps out of my chest. Finally, a little bit of information.

"Oh, yeah? You're boss is a woman?"

"Yeah."

"Is she a badass like you?"

"That's an understatement."

I smile. "What's her name?"

"Oksana."

"Oksana," I repeat. My skin is buzzing. "Russian?"

"Ukrainian. We call her the Crazy Ukrainian."

I laugh. "Okay, so I'll talk to the Crazy Ukrainian as soon as possible and offer to pay her thirty thousand in fees to reserve your time exclusively for the next couple weeks—and since that will be separate from my club membership, I'll tell them my payment is conditioned on them splitting the pot with you fifty-fifty. How does that sound?"

Stacy looks closer to climaxing now than she did when we fucked. "Oh," she says, her cheeks flushing. "Why do you even need to deal with Oksana? Why not just pay the whole amount to me directly under the table? She doesn't need to know. Just give me the money, and I give you my word—all my time for two weeks, every minute of every day and night if you want. I'll fuck you so good, you won't want our two weeks to end."

Déjà vu. Didn't Julia Roberts say something eerily similar to that at the beginning of *Pretty Woman*? "No, that won't work. If you're suddenly not showing up for other check-ins, won't they figure something's up?"

She nods, reluctantly. "Yeah, probably. But you could just check-in and request me every day, and then pay me the cash directly. It's a win-win-win all around."

Shit. "Hmm. The whole point is I don't want to do the check-in thing. And, anyway, you're sure to get a bunch of other requests during that two weeks—I have to believe you're their top requested girl."

She smirks. "I am."

"I don't want to risk even the chance of sharing you while I'm with you. If we're sneaky about it and they find out somehow, things could really backfire. You might lose your job and The Club might ban me for the rest of my membership period. I absolutely can't risk that. I need this club, Stacy." I flash her my crazy eyes.

She twists her mouth, obviously trying to figure out a way to maximize her take. "I'll take a 'vacation' for a couple weeks—to visit a sick relative or something."

"How about I make sure you wind up with thirty thousand for the two weeks, no matter what?

She nods profusely.

"But I'd still like to do it above-board. I'll pay The Club whatever I have to pay, over and above your fee, to make it work. Does that sound good?"

Her eyes light up. "Perfect."

Jesus. I should hire Stacy to negotiate one of my business deals. She's a fucking shark. "So do you think Oksana will go for it? Is she the decision-maker, or is she gonna have to clear this with someone else?"

"Why wouldn't she go for it? It's all about the Benjamins with her—and, yeah, what Oksana says goes. I told you—she's a badass."

"Great. So how do I contact her?"

"Give me your phone number. I'll tell her to call you." She pulls out her phone.

"No, I'd prefer to contact Oksana. I like being in control in matters such as this—well, in all matters, actually." Just for my own amusement, I flash her my crazy eyes again.

"I'm not allowed to give out her number."

"Is she here in Seattle?"

"No, Las Vegas."

My skin sizzles. *Oksana the Ukrainian in Las Vegas.*

"What's her last name?"

Stacy looks at me sideways. "Why?"

I hold up my phone. "Just wanted to put her in my phone. Is that not allowed?" I play dumb.

There's a beat.

"You don't need her last name."

I pushed it too far. "I'm sorry, I didn't know. This is all new to me. I've never had a GFE before. You know what? I have some business in Vegas, anyway. I'll kill two birds with one stone and pay her in person in cash so she can pay you right away. Do you have her physical address?"

I've said the magic word. *Cash.* Her eyes light up. "All I've got is a P.O. box in Vegas. I'll give you her email address. You can contact her and figure out how to connect."

"Great."

She grabs a pen out of her purse. "I need a piece of paper." She rummages in her bag.

"You've met Oksana in person, I presume?"

"Oh yeah, I started this job in Vegas. I was on the first team of girls, before they branched out to other cities."

Another kernel of information. Las Vegas is their mother ship.

"I was their top girl in Vegas—most requested." She smiles with pride. "When they expanded operations, they gave me my pick of cities," she says.

"And you picked Seattle?"

"I was tired of the dry heat."

"Well, you certainly solved that problem by coming here, huh?"

She smiles. "And I've got family here in Seattle, so . . ."

We sit and stare at each other for a moment in awkward silence. She suddenly looks years younger to me than she did just a moment ago.

"Oksana?" I say, gently prodding her to stay on task and give me that email address.

"Oh, yeah," she says. "Sure thing."

"I'll just input her email address onto my phone." My stomach hurts. I feel like I'm betraying Sarah. And, frankly, I'm taking no pleasure in scamming Stacy the Faker. I just want to be done with this and go home to Sarah.

"Okay." She opens her list of contacts on her phone and scrolls down.

I type the name "Oksana" into my contacts and look up, ready for her to tell me the email address. "Okay, what's the address?"

"Jonas?"

Oh God, no.

Panic floods me like a tidal wave.

This is my worst nightmare.

And my own damned fault.

It's Sarah.

Chapter 13
Sarah

I look at my watch. Five minutes to seven.

I shouldn't be doing this right now—I know I shouldn't. But I can't help myself.

The tip of my nose is cold and turning red in the chilly night air. I hug my sweatshirt to me and keep walking briskly toward The Pine Box. My heart bangs in my chest. I shouldn't be doing this. But I pick up my pace, anyway.

After Jonas left the house, I called Kat to make sure no dancing hitmen had paid her a visit today.

"I'm great," she said. "I'm about to grab dinner with my *bodyguard*." And then she belted out Whitney Houston's famous chorus from *The Bodyguard*.

"What are you talking about?" I asked, laughing.

"Jonas didn't tell you? He hired a professional bodyguard to watch over me. Please tell him thank you, by the way—my hunky bodyguard is way cuter than Kevin Costner."

I was stunned at Jonas' thoughtfulness, yet again, but also anxious to think he deemed a bodyguard a necessary precaution.

"Do you and Jonas want to meet us for dinner?" Kat asked.

"Not tonight. I've got to study and Jonas is out."

"What's he up to?" she asked. "Working?"

"I don't know. He just said he had something he had to do."

Kat responded with a kind of wincing noise that spoke volumes about her mistrust of Jonas.

"What?" I asked.

"Nothing."

"Jonas and I have been joined at the hip since he picked me up for Belize"—quite often *literally* joined at the hip, I thought, smirking—"and now he's all stressed out about protecting me from the bad guys. Poor guy, I'm sure he just needed a little space."

Kat didn't reply.

I grunted with exasperation. "Just say whatever it is you're thinking."

She sighed. "The guy joined a sex club not too long ago, remember. If he were my boyfriend, I'd want to know what he was doing, that's all."

"You don't know him like I do," I assured her. "He's not the dog you think he is."

"I don't think he's a dog. But he's not a perfect angel, either. I'm just saying, if Jonas Faraday were my boyfriend, I'd want to know where he was."

Two minutes later, I was clutching that goddamned Club iPhone in my hand like a frickin' grenade, having found it in only the third drawer I'd opened in the kitchen. Just holding it in my hand made me sick. Until it appeared on the kitchen table this morning, I'd assumed Jonas had gotten rid of the hideous thing after his disastrous night with Stacy the Faker, or, at the very latest, after he'd offered me exclusive membership in the Jonas Faraday Club. Why the hell did he keep it? And if he'd kept the iPhone, I couldn't help reasoning, did that mean he'd kept the purple bracelet, too? I searched for the bracelet in the same drawer where I'd found the iPhone, but it wasn't there, which meant he'd thrown the dastardly thing away, thank goodness—or, I suddenly thought, my heart leaping into my throat, that he was wearing it at that very moment. The latter possibility made my flesh crawl. And my heart ache. And the marrow in my *Fatal-Attraction* bone start simmering. The mere thought of Jonas wearing that frickin' purple bracelet on his wrist, right alongside the Belizian friendship bracelet that matches mine, made me want to boil a little white bunny in a pot.

Opening the iPhone to confirm or debunk my fears wasn't possible—the damned thing was fingerprint- and passcode-protected—and so, in a fit of anger, I threw it with a loud clank into the big trashcan in the garage. And that's when I saw Jonas' car parked in the garage, the engine cold—which made me flip out even further. Either someone had picked Jonas up to take him wherever he'd gone—not a comforting thought—or, in the alternative, he'd *walked* there—also not a comforting thought, in light of a conversation Jonas and I had had in Belize.

We'd been lying in bed in our tree house after making love for the umpteenth time that day, laughing, sharing secrets, divulging our most awkward and cringe-worthy moments. No topic was off limits. We'd told each other about our respective de-virginizations. We'd talked about our past relationships. I'd told him about my two one-night stands, and how ill prepared I'd been for the inevitable brush-offs afterwards, and he'd said he wanted to beat those assholes up for me. And then Jonas had told me a few selected anecdotes from his illustrious career as a shameless man-whore.

"But how did you *find* all those willing women?" I asked, incredulous. "Did you just snap your fingers or what?"

"Well, yeah, most often, they approached me. Other times, I just walked to The Pine Box," he said, "and it was like shooting ducks in a barrel. The bar being walking distance from my house made saying goodbye afterwards super easy—no second car to juggle."

"Wow, you were such a pig," I said.

"I prefer asshole-motherfucker," he said.

"You'll hear no argument from me."

I laughed and kissed him and we made love yet again, the howler monkeys in the trees serenading us all the while.

I keep walking toward The Pine Box, picking up my pace yet again. I'm shivering in the cool night air. I wish I'd grabbed my North Face jacket from my apartment when Jonas and I were there this morning. Damn.

He's not going to be in the bar, I tell myself. *You're wasting your time acting like a clingy, insecure lunatic when you should be studying.*

I know.

He probably just went to the rock climbing gym to blow off some steam.

Then why wasn't he wearing workout clothes when he left the house?

Maybe he had a gym bag in his car.

His car is sitting in his garage.

He probably just needed a drink.

113

There's a six-pack of beer in his fridge.

Stop being paranoid. You love him, Sarah. And he loves you. Madness, remember?

Of course, I remember. It's all I think about, day and night. Yes, I love him—so much it hurts. And he loves me—I'm sure of it.

Then why the hell are you walking to The Pine Box right now?

Why the hell did he keep that *fucking* iPhone?

I don't know.

And if he kept the iPhone, then isn't it logical to think he kept the purple bracelet, too?

Logical, yes. Probable, no.

Regardless, why did he keep the iPhone in the first place?

Pick up the pace.

It's official. I'm schizophrenic.

Fifty feet away from the bar, I stop dead in my tracks. Stacy the Faker stands in front of the bar in a short black dress, feeding quarters into a parking meter. It's definitely her. I'd know her anywhere.

I can't breathe.

When Stacy finishes with the meter, she turns around and marches into The Pine Box, her impossibly long legs leading the way on her impossibly high stiletto heels.

I sprint to the back window of the bar and peek inside, clutching my chest. I scan the crowded bar through the window.

Maybe he's not in there. Maybe this is just a crazy coincidence. Maybe Stacy's here to meet some other guy from The Club. Maybe—

In an instant, all the "maybes" bouncing around in my head vanish. There he is, standing at the bar, drinking a beer. *Jonas.* My sweet Jonas. Or so I thought.

Stacy approaches him. Jonas hugs her, albeit awkwardly.

My stomach lurches.

I can't breathe.

My head spins.

This makes no sense. Jonas loves me. I can't wrap my brain around what I'm seeing. Tears well up in my eyes. A lump rises in my throat.

Jonas motions to the bartender. The bartender nods.

I can't understand what I'm seeing. This makes no sense. Jonas said he fucked Stacy and the whole time imagined she was me—and this was even before he knew what I looked like. That's what he told me, anyway. He said she faked it with him—that she repulsed him—that he literally gagged—that the whole experience disgusted him. And now he wants to fuck her again? Even though she *faked* it with him?

My eyes widen with my horrifying epiphany.

Stacy faked it with him.

Oh my God.

What did Jonas write in his application about that woman who faked it with him before—the one who unwittingly inspired his lingual quest for alleged truth and honesty in the first place? "I wanted to teach her a lesson about truth and honesty," he wrote, "but even more than that, I wanted *redemption.*"

Oh my God. I think I'm going to barf.

I can barely see Jonas and Stacy through my tears. I wipe my eyes.

They turn away from the bar, looking for an open table. Stacy motions in the direction of "my" table—the one where Kat and I spied on Jonas and Stacy the first time—oh Lord have mercy, I can't believe there's now a *first* time—but after brief discussion they move in the opposite direction to another table.

I scoot around the corner of the bar to gain a better vantage point of them through another window.

Stacy faked it with him, and now he can't resist her. He's an addict and she's his smack, loaded into a syringe and positioned right into his vein. He can't resist shooting her up, regardless of whether he loves me or not. Would loving me change a goddamned thing if he were a heroin addict? No, it wouldn't. An addict needs his fix—loved ones be damned. And this is Jonas Faraday's fix. I knew it from day one, but I wanted to believe I could change him. I thought I was his rehab, his savior, but I was deluding myself. He held off as long as he could. He tried.

Tears squirt out of my eyes.

I grab at my hair and pull on it. I'm out of my head right now. My heart physically aches inside my chest cavity. I've never felt so lost, so alone, so betrayed in all my life. So heartbroken.

When Jonas fucked Stacy the Faker and wished she were me, sight unseen, before he'd ever laid a magical finger on me, well, that was hot,

hot, hot—but Jonas fucking Stacy after all that's happened between us, after all we've said and done and *felt*, after everything we've told each other, after that kiss outside the cave in Belize, after all the times we've made love, after all the times I've "surrendered" to him, and jumped off a frickin' waterfall for him, and the bracelets he put on our wrists—oh my God, holy fuckballs, the bracelets!—well, after all that, Jonas fucking Stacy the Faker is a different kind of *hot*—the kind of hot you get when you burn down your boyfriend's fucking house.

My chest heaves.

My mind feels like it's detaching from my body, and not in the way Jonas always refers to—I feel my sanity slipping away. I imagine myself walking in there and slapping Jonas across his gorgeous fucking face and telling him to go to fucking hell. But the thought makes my heart seize and twist and burn. I thought he loved me the way I love him. I thought we'd discovered a mutual madness.

I've got a serious mental disease, he told me.

No shit, you do, Jonas Fucking Faraday. Even after everything we've been through together, you kept that damned iPhone so you could fuck a prostitute who—

I stand completely upright, suddenly having a lightning bolt of a thought. I cock my head like a cockatiel. Hang on a second. This doesn't make any sense.

Hang on a cotton pickin' second.

This doesn't add up.

Jonas would never fuck a prostitute.

I squint through the window and peer at him. He's talking, smiling, looking as gorgeous as ever. He swigs his beer.

He's not wearing his purple bracelet.

I'm frozen on the sidewalk in the cold night air.

Jonas would never fuck a prostitute.

I saw the way Jonas reacted on the airplane when I told him about my encounter with Stacy in the sports bar—how it tortured him to realize he'd unknowingly brought a hooker into his bed. He became physically ill. Mortified. Humiliated. Angry. He wasn't faking that reaction—it was real. And in Belize, on that first magical, sexless night, he sobbed into my arms as he told me about his father's self-destructive obsession with prostitutes during the year before his suicide. Jonas called his father's behavior "disgusting."

I'm shaking, adrenaline coursing through me.

Jonas would never knowingly sleep with a prostitute. Sex is the ultimate expression of honesty to him. Ergo, paying a woman to *pretend* to "surrender" to him would be antithetical to everything he stands for. It would *repel* him, not turn him on.

Inside the bar, two big guys stand up from their table, blocking my view of Jonas and Stacy. I move to the next window, just in time to see Stacy bat her eyelashes at something Jonas has said to her. Obviously, he just paid her a compliment.

What the fuck is going on here? He's up to something, yes. But cheating on me with Stacy the Prostitute? No. What the hell is he doing?

Think, Sarah, think. Think like Jonas.

Stacy reaches across the table and puts her hand on Jonas'. He jerks his hand away like her hand burned his skin. He tries to make it seem like he's grabbing his beer, but oh my God, it's plain as day he can't stand to be touched by her.

I smile. Oh, Jonas. Sweet Jonas. Stupid-Lying-Idiotic Jonas. You're-In-Such-Big-Trouble Jonas. But, yes, undoubtedly, Faithful Jonas.

What could he possibly be saying to her?

Think, Sarah, think.

He had the iPhone out this morning during his conversation with Josh. When I asked about it, he said he wanted to handle The Club on his own, with Josh, and leave me out of it.

I roll my eyes. Oh good God. He's here to get information out of Stacy—and he's charming her to do it. He's complimenting her, telling her what she wants to hear—all so he can gather information for his highfalutin *strategy*, whatever the hell it is. I wipe my eyes. He's just trying to protect me, the big dummy.

Relief ripples through every muscle of my body.

I'm still pissed, though. He may not be a cheater, but he's still an idiot. A big, fat idiot. And a liar through omission. He should have included me in his plans from minute one. What does he think—I'm too fragile and innocent, or maybe not smart enough, to handle his stupid strategy? That I'm going to come undone? I've been doing research and investigations professionally for the last three months, buddy! I figure shit out, man! Who tracked you down tonight like a

117

hungry crack whore looking for her baby daddy on payday? Me! And, anyway, I'm the one who was employed by The Club, for the love of all things holy—doesn't he think I might have an idea or two to contribute to his stupid *strategy*, whatever it is? God, I hate Strategic Jonas! Strategic Jonas makes me want to punch him in his beautiful face.

I take a deep breath and watch them, my nostrils flaring.

Whatever he's saying, she's buying it hook-line-and-sinker. She's nodding vigorously. She stands, smiling at him like she expects him to get up with her.

But he doesn't move.

She sits back down, perplexed.

Oh, Jonas.

I smile.

I'm one hundred percent sure he's not here to fuck Stacy. If he were, they'd already be fucking up a storm somewhere. My sweet Jonas is a lot of things, including a dumbass, apparently, and a liar, and an idiot, but a man who sits around drinking a beer and chatting with a prostitute when all he wants to do is fuck, he is not. I can't help but laugh out loud. For a smart man, my sweet Jonas is such a big dummy sometimes, I swear to God.

Chapter 14
Jonas

"Jonas?"

Oh God, no.

Panic floods me like a tidal wave.

This is my worst nightmare.

And my own damned fault.

It's Sarah.

Her eyes are red and wet. Tear tracks stain her cheeks.

"Sarah." That's all I can eek out. This can't be happening right now. This is my worst nightmare. My heart explodes in my chest.

Stacy lifts her wineglass to her lips, a smug smile spreading across her face.

"Sarah," I say again. "Please—"

"There's nothing to say. I know exactly why you're here."

"No, you don't. Please listen." I glance at Stacy. She's grinning like a Cheshire cat.

"You had 'something you needed to do,' huh?"

My stomach leaps into my mouth. My tongue isn't working.

"*Sarah*, is it?" Stacy interjects. "Jonas was just telling me about your problem with emotional attachment—"

"Shut the fuck up, Stacy," Sarah hisses. Her eyes are laser beams.

Stacy smirks, apparently unfazed.

"Stacy, will you excuse us for just a minute, please?" I say, my voice sounding much calmer than I feel.

"No, Stacy, stay here, please," Sarah says. "I want you to hear this."

I stand and grab Sarah's arm. "Sarah, listen to me."

119

She jerks away from me. "Sit down. I have something to say to you both."

My mouth hangs open. I'm going to have a fucking heart attack. I can't lose her. Not like this. Please, God, no. I'm officially in hell. "No, listen, I'm—" I reach for her again.

Sarah jerks away again. "If you don't take your hands off me right now and sit the fuck down, I'm walking out that door, Jonas."

Shit. Oh God. This is a catastrophe. I'm light-headed. I sit.

"All I've ever heard from you since day one was Stacy this and Stacy that," Sarah begins, seething.

What? What the fuck is she saying? Yeah, during our very first phone call, I told her about my horrible fuck with Stacy, but—

"And what a 'smokin' hot body' she has . . ."

Oh my God, no. This is crazy. Last night I said Stacy has a smokin' hot body, yes, but only so Josh and I could compare notes about his Seattle girl—

"All I ever hear is Stacy, Stacy, Stacy—how great Stacy is in bed."

Wait, what? Have I had a psychotic break and I don't know it?

Sarah glares at Stacy. "Do you know how many times he's said to me, 'Why can't you fuck me the way Stacy did'?"

The universe warps and buckles and slows to a screeching halt.

Sarah flashes me her patented I'm-smarter-than-you smirk.

Holy shit. She knows. She understands. Oh my God. How the fuck did she figure this out? How did she know I'd be here tonight? And why does she know exactly what line of bullshit I've been slinging to Stacy? A smile threatens my lips, but I suppress it. She's the most amazing woman in the world. Holy shit, she's the woman of my dreams.

Sarah whips her head and glares at Stacy again. "Well, guess what, Stacy—or Cassandra, or whatever your name is—you've fucked with the wrong woman. Jonas Faraday is *mine*—my territory, my score—and I don't need anybody making a play for my sloppy seconds." She leans right into Stacy's face, her eyes narrowed to slits. "Don't fuck with me, bitch."

I can't speak. She's magnificent.

Stacy rises to her feet, ready to rumble.

I get up, too, ready to intercede.

But Sarah doesn't back down. She grits her teeth. "I've written a detailed report about The Club and I've addressed it to the Federal Bureau of Investigation, the U.S. Attorney's Office, and, given The Club's roster of members, the U.S. Secret Service, too."

Stacy's eyes widen. Sarah just called her bluff.

There's a long beat.

"Take a seat, asshole," Sarah says firmly. "Please."

Stacy sits.

And so do I. I'm not sure which one of us she just called an asshole.

Sarah takes the seat next to me and leans forward across the table.

"I've got a message for whoever's running The Club, and I want you to deliver it for me."

Stacy clenches her jaw.

"Tell them I'm not currently planning to send my report to anyone. Frankly, I don't care what The Club does and I'd take no pleasure in publicly humiliating members or their families. But if anything happens to me, or to my friend Kat, or to this man here, or to anyone I care about, if The Club fucks with me or my people in any way, then each of those law enforcement agencies will *immediately* receive that report. I've already made detailed arrangements through multiple resources. It's all set."

Stacy leans back, her face flushed.

"My report is some damned good reading, too, lemme tell you. We're talking hundreds of counts of prostitution and sex trafficking and money laundering under both state and federal laws, plus Internet fraud, wire fraud, racketeering—jeez, I'm guessing a good federal prosecutor could come up with at least a hundred counts under RICO alone—and then there's good old fashioned theft and fraud under state laws, too."

Stacy's nostrils flare.

"I realize it's gonna be hard for you to convey the specifics of my message to the powers that be, Stacy, so just give them the gist and tell them to give me a call. I'd be happy to explain everything in explicit detail."

I'm transfixed. I've never witnessed such an erotic blend of power and beauty and brains in all my life. She's stunning—a goddess—a fucking superhero. Orgasma the All-Powerful, indeed.

"And I've also got a personal message for you, too, Stacy—woman to woman. Fuck you." Sarah smiles. "Whatever you and Jonas talked about isn't gonna happen. He's *mine*." She looks at me. "Tell her you're mine."

"I'm hers."

"I'm not gunning to take you down, Stacy. A girl's got to make a living. You can have anybody but Jonas, any lonely moneybags-wack-job in the greater Seattle area—in the whole world, for all I care. I don't give a fuck. All I care about is this man right here. You got that?"

Stacy swallows but doesn't speak. Her eyes are chips of blue granite.

Sarah smooths an errant hair away from her face and juts her chin in my direction. "Jonas?"

"Yes, Sarah?"

"I'm going to fuck you now—and you don't even have to pay me to do it."

"Thank you."

"I won't do it the way Stacy did it, of course."

"Of course."

"But I'll give it my best shot."

I almost burst out laughing.

"Jonas?"

"Yes?"

"Say goodbye to Stacy."

"Goodbye, Stacy." I stand and pull my wallet out of my jeans pocket. I throw six hundred-dollar bills onto the table in front of her. "Your usual fee plus a twenty-percent tip," I explain politely. I wink.

Stacy's eye twitches.

I grab Sarah's hand and pull her to a stand beside me. "Come on, baby. Let's go fuck each other's brains out."

Chapter 15
Sarah

"So. Fucking. Hot. So. Fucking. Hot. So. Fucking. Hot." Each word he barks at me is accompanied by a zealous thrust of his body.

He's fucking my brains out against the filthy wall of the men's bathroom.

I'm so mad at him right now, I don't even want to speak to him. But fuck him? Yes. As mad as I am, when he said, "Come on, baby, let's go fuck each other's brains out," *right in front of Stacy the Faker,* holy moly, the moment was too scorching hot not to capitalize on it. Every so often, a girl's gotta treat herself to a little I'm-so-pissed-at-you sex. There's nothing quite like it.

"Oh, baby, you fucking killed it," he groans. "So. Fucking. Hot." His thrusts are wildly enthusiastic. "Did you see her face when you told her about the report? So. Fucking. Hot. So. Fucking. Smart." He punctuates each word with another beastly thrust. "So. Fucking. Smart. Oh, Baby. My baby. Oh, Sarah."

His lips devour my mouth.

I'm dangerously close to completely letting go and losing my mind in a whole new, dirty, dirty way. But, no, I'm so mad at him, so hurt, so betrayed, I'm not going to come this time, just to prove my point. It shouldn't be hard to stop myself, for Pete's sake—this bathroom is utterly disgusting. What the hell am I doing in here? I cannot believe I'm having sex in the men's bathroom of a bar. I'm such a dirty, dirty girl. Oh, wow, I just made myself hot. Dirty, dirty girl. Oh God, yes, yes, yes, yes, yes, this feels so good. Dirty, dirty girl. Ow, my head just slammed loudly against the wall.

He stops abruptly, wincing. "Are you okay?"

"Yeah. Don't stop. Come on. Yes, yes, yes." I growl my words

123

loudly and Jonas responds with vigor. "You're in so much trouble," I snarl at him. "You're in so much fucking trouble."

"I know," he says. "I was so bad."

"So bad. Fuck me harder."

"You want it hard?"

"As hard as you can give it to me. Is that all you got?" I stifle a scream.

His hand gropes my breast. His lips suck on mine. His face is covered in sweat. His body heat is palpable.

"I'm gonna get you off and I'm not gonna come myself," I growl. "Just to punish you. You were bad. So. Bad. So. Bad. I'm. Not. Gonna. Come."

"Oh, you're gonna come, baby. Oh, fuck, you feel so good. You like it when I fuck you, baby?"

"That's all you got?"

"You want more?"

"I want all you got."

"Oh God, Sarah. So fucking smart, baby. So. Fucking. Smart. You're a fucking genius."

"And you're a fucking idiot."

He laughs and groans at the same time.

"Turn around," he orders.

I don't obey.

He forcefully turns me around and spreads my legs like he's frisking me. I place my palms on the nasty bathroom wall. He continues fucking me from behind as his fingers reach around and touch me. I'm so wet, so fucking wet, I should be wearing rain boots. Holy mother of God.

"You're not gonna come, huh?" he asks. He bites my neck.

"No." I shudder and moan.

"To teach me a lesson?"

I can't verbalize a response. His fingers are working me with too much skill. I'm delirious.

He growls loudly. He's close.

"Say it," I moan loudly.

He knows exactly what I want. "I'm yours."

Tell her you're mine, I said to him in front of Stacy. *I'm hers,* he said, as if we'd rehearsed it. *I'm hers,* he told her—and her face turned bright red.

That's right. Fuck you, Stacy. He's mine. *Mine, mine, mine, mine.* Oh, God, yes. Yes, yes, yes. I'm fluttering, rippling, close to the edge. I groan loudly.

"Again," I order him. This wall is disgusting. I'm a dirty, dirty girl.

"I'm yours."

"Again." I can't breathe.

"I'm yours. Yours. Yours. Yours. Oh, Sarah. Yours. Yours. Oh, God, Sarah. I'm yours."

"Jonas." The sound that emerges from me is quite similar to the sound I'd make if I were in this filthy bathroom praying to the porcelain gods after one too many mojitos (a comparison I'm unfortunately able to draw through actual experience). I'm splitting into two with my ecstasy. My body is rending, wretching, heaving in painful pleasure—or maybe my body's just reacting to the foul bathroom wall.

Oh yes, oh God, yes, I'm definitely coming. And hard. Motherfucker, I can't help myself. This is just too hot. I let out a guttural growl.

He climaxes right on my heels, letting out a strangled cry of his own.

Holy shit, this bathroom is utterly nauseating.

He collapses onto my back, a sweaty, savage heap.

Damn, that was hot. So. Fucking. Hot.

And I'm so mad at him I could cry. In fact, now that my adrenaline is rapidly receding, I very well might do just that. I tilt my pelvis away from him to force him out of me. I turn around and glare at him.

He smiles broadly: the cat that swallowed the canary.

"You're so fucking hot," he says simply.

Without saying a word, I pull up my panties, push down my skirt, and scrub my arms and hands and face in the sink with hot water. And then, after quickly drying myself with a paper towel, I bolt out the bathroom door. Jonas follows silently behind me.

Some guy stands outside the door of the one-room bathroom as we depart, waiting to go inside.

"She was sick, man," Jonas says in passing. "Sorry."

"Yeah. Sick of waiting around for this asshole-motherfucker to *fuck* me," I say. I don't know why I say it, but I do.

The guy bursts out laughing and so does Jonas.

"Nice," the guy says to Jonas.

I march into the bar area, with Jonas following mutely behind me. I steal a glance at the booth where Jonas and I sat only minutes ago with Stacy the Fucking Faker. She's long gone. Good. Run along and tell your bosses every word I said. *Bitch.*

I beeline over to the bar. "Two shots of Patron," I say to the bartender, gesturing to Jonas and myself.

Jonas stares at me, smirking, but not speaking.

The bartender pours the shots.

"Jonas?"

"Yes, Sarah."

"Pay the man," I say.

Jonas pulls out his wallet and lays down the cash.

I knock back the shot and bite into my lime. I stare at Jonas, defiant. I'm so mad at him, I don't want to speak to him right now.

"You are so fucking hot," he says. He throws back his shot and bites his lime.

I glance to the other end of the bar and gasp. There's a guy at the far end of the bar, staring at me—and, holy crappola, he looks just like John Travolta. Granted, John Travolta from *Look Who's Talking, Too,* but still. I clutch Jonas and he instantly puts his arm around me, sensing my sudden anxiety.

I nudge Jonas' arm. "Jonas, look," I whisper. I motion with my head to the end of the bar.

He looks in the direction I've indicated. "What?"

"Is that him? The John Travolta guy?"

Jonas looks again, squeezing me tight, trying to understand what I'm talking about. His grip on my body is so forceful that it hurts.

"Blue shirt," I whisper.

Jonas focuses on the target and relaxes his grip. "Oh my God, Sarah, come on. You really think that guy looks anything like Vincent Vega?"

"Who the hell is Vincent Vega?" I shake my head. "Is that the John Travolta guy you saw earlier today?"

"'*Who the hell is Vincent Vega?*' Oh my God, you haven't actually seen *Pulp Fiction,* have you?"

"Of course, I have. Never mind. I'm pissed at you. I can't even talk to you right now." Sudden emotion wells up inside me and catches in my throat. Tonight has been a horrible, wretched, death-defying mind fuck. Without another word, I turn away from him and bolt out of the bar.

Chapter 16
Sarah

Jonas hoots into the chilly night air as we walk away from the bar. He keeps leaping into the air like he's doing some sort of touchdown dance. "You were amazing, baby! Holy shit! A fucking genius! And so fucking hot!"

My legs wobble. I'm still flushed with adrenaline and anger and hurt. "I'm not in the mood to celebrate," I mutter, my hand on my chest, steadying myself.

He sweeps me up and cradles me in his arms, just like he did after I jumped off the waterfall in Belize. "I've got you," he says, kissing my cheek. He's jubilant. "You kicked ass in there. Oh my God. Orgasma the All-Powerful strikes again!" He laughs and hoots again.

I don't want to be cuddled by Jonas right now. I'm angry at him. "Put me down. I'm mad at you."

He laughs.

"Jonas, I'm not kidding. Put me down. I'm really, really mad. And hurt."

He puts me down, elation draining from his face like water swirling down a toilet bowl.

I march ahead of him, trying to collect my thoughts.

"You know I only met Stacy to gather information—"

"Yeah, I know."

"You can't possibly think I wanted to—"

"I don't." I quicken my pace. I'm furious. And hurt. And just plain confused.

"Sarah, I would never, ever—"

"Jonas, just give me a minute. I'm so pissed at you, I can't even speak. Just don't talk."

I can feel him bursting at the seams behind me, but he grants my request—for a solid forty seconds.

"Sarah," he finally says. "I can't stand it. Talk to me."

I stop walking and whip around to look at him, tears in my eyes.

"Oh, baby," he begins, reaching for me. But I cut him off.

"I should be studying right now!" I shriek. "Only the top ten students get a scholarship!" I burst into tears. "I need that scholarship, Jonas, and I haven't studied for a whole *week,* thanks to you." This isn't at all what's foremost on my mind. I have no idea why this is what my brain chose to barf out at this moment. I choke down the sob that threatens to rise from my throat.

He moves to comfort me again, but I put my hands up.

"Don't. I'm so mad at you right now I can't see straight."

He opens his mouth to say something but stops himself.

"I'm a grown-ass woman, Jonas. I'm strong. I'm smart. You should have told me what you were up to. I can handle it—I can *help.* But you didn't trust me enough to tell me the truth."

"It's not an issue of trust. I didn't tell you because I wanted to keep you out of harm's way."

"Bullshit."

He raises his eyebrows.

"You didn't tell me because you didn't trust me not to fuck up your precious strategy, whatever the hell it is."

He rolls his eyes. "No, Sarah, that's not it."

"If tonight were reversed, you'd be just as pissed as I am right now, probably more so."

"You're reading way too much into this."

"Really? Think about it. If I checked in on the Club app without telling you and secretly met up with a guy—*a guy I'd fucked once before*—what would you do?"

He clenches his jaw.

"You think you might wig out just a little bit? Or at least wonder why the *fuck* I didn't tell you?"

He exhales.

"What if I said, 'Oh, don't worry, Jonas, I wasn't gonna *fuck* him, you silly goose—yes, he happens to be the last guy I fucked before I met you, but I was just planning to make him *think* I wanted to fuck him for this super-duper awesome strategy I have—a super-duper awesome strategy I've told you nothing about.'"

He glares at me.

"And what if we add one more little fact to this hypothetical. What if I'd slept with a different guy every single night for the past year—right up until I met you? And then I ran off to a check-in with the very last guy I'd been with? You're telling me you wouldn't wonder just a teeny-tiny little bit what the *fuck* I was doing when I said I had 'something I had to do' tonight?"

He smashes his lips together.

"Ya feeling me on this?" My chest is heaving. Damn, I'm furious. He doesn't understand how close he came to smashing my heart into a million pieces tonight.

There's a long beat.

"I'm a dumbshit," he finally says quietly.

"Felony stupid," I agree.

He looks defeated.

"The problem isn't you meeting up with Stacy. I get what you were trying to do—whatever the hell it was. The problem is you not *telling* me about it—not trusting me enough to tell me."

He sighs. There's a long beat.

"My imagination started playing tricks on me tonight, Jonas." I sigh. "That's why I went to the bar in the first place." Tears well up in my eyes. "Paranoia got the best of me. When I saw your car parked in the garage, I remembered how you said you used to walk to The Pine Box on your 'hunting expeditions' . . ." I wipe my eyes.

He's instantly indignant. "You thought I went to the bar to pick someone up? To *fuck* someone?"

"I thought it was possible."

"How could you think that, even for a second?"

I give him a "duh" look.

"After everything I've—" He shakes his head. "After Belize? After last night? That's what you think of me?"

I glance away.

"I'd never do that to you. Look at me."

I look at him.

"Don't you know you fucking own me?"

"You kept The Club's iPhone."

"To give to Trey."

130

"It was on the table this morning."

"Because I'm figuring out how to fuck The Club up the ass—to protect my beautiful, precious baby. Everything I do is to protect you. I'm telling you, Sarah, you own me."

"Stop saying that. I don't *own* you."

"Yes, you do."

"No, I don't. If I *owned* you, as you allege, you would have told me what you were up to."

He exhales in exasperation. There's another long beat.

"If I truly *owned* you, there wouldn't have been room for doubt in my mind. By keeping things from me, you left room for me to doubt."

His face is etched with pain.

"Jonas, tonight was horrible. My heart was a whisper away from shattering. I started thinking maybe you couldn't resist teaching Stacy the Faker a lesson about truth and honesty—getting your *redemption* the second time around."

His eyes burst into flames. "How could you think that?"

"Oh, gee! Maybe because I saw you sitting in a bar having drinks with her—*and you didn't tell me about it!*"

He throws up his hands, totally pissed. "Jesus."

"And then I thought, 'Oh, wait, no, Jonas would never fuck a *prostitute.*'"

He nods emphatically, like I'm finally making some sense.

"But that's the problem right there. I shouldn't have been thinking, 'Jonas would never cheat on me with a prostitute.' I should have been thinking, 'Jonas would never cheat on me, period, with anyone.'"

He runs his hand through his hair. "I thought we were done with this. Remember what we said in Belize? Full steam ahead? No more one step forward, two steps back? No more trust issues. You promised."

"Yeah, and we *were* done with this. I kept my promise. I trusted you—completely—until you gave me a reason to doubt you."

He shakes his head.

"Secrets create spaces within a relationship, Jonas—dark spaces. When one person keeps secrets, the other person fills in the dark spaces with their fears and insecurities."

He stares at me for a long beat. "That's profound, actually."

"Thanks. I made it up. Just now. On the spot."

"I like it. It makes a lot of sense." He shoots me a half-smile. "You're pretty fucking smart, you know that?"

I shrug. Tears threaten my eyes.

"Sarah, I do trust you. More than I've ever trusted any woman, ever. I've told you things . . ." He sighs. "I've opened myself up to you in whole new ways."

I shiver in the cold. "Let's keep walking. It's frickin' freezing."

He puts his arm around me as we walk. He's warm. His arm around me is strong. He smells delicious, even after he's just had sweaty sex in a men's bathroom. His physicality is so alluring to me, such a welcome distraction from the rambling dialogue inside my head, I'm tempted to blurt, "Never mind" and just kiss him. But sweeping my emotions under the carpet won't solve anything. It only means they'll come out later, and probably with a vengeance. We need to have this conversation now.

"You made me jump off a frickin' waterfall, Jonas," I say. "And I'm deathly afraid of heights."

He smiles. "I know."

"This whole relationship has been about *me*. Making *me* let go. Making *me* 'surrender.' What about you?"

He doesn't reply.

"You're fucked up, too, you know."

"Royally."

"Well, what's your waterfall? When are *you* gonna jump off a waterfall for *me*?"

We walk in silence for a minute longer.

He stops short all of a sudden. He pulls me into him and kisses me. His nose is cold against mine, but his lips are warm. He abruptly pulls away from me and cups my face in his hands.

"This. This right here," he whispers. "Every single minute I'm with you, I'm jumping off a waterfall. Don't you understand?" His eyes burn with intensity. "You're afraid of heights? Well, I'm afraid of *this*. I'm standing on a cliff a hundred feet tall, and every day with you, I jump. I don't know how to do this, okay? It's all new to me— and I'm terrible at it. So, okay, I'm gonna fuck things up sometimes. But... " He swallows hard, suppressing his emotions. "But every day,

I see your beautiful face, every day I get to touch your smooth skin and kiss your spectacular lips and make love to you—oh my God—and talk to you and laugh with you and tell you things I've never told anyone else, *ever*—all of it makes me want to keep climbing higher and higher to the next waterfall, to the next day, and just keep jumping and jumping and jumping into the abyss." He's shaking. "With you."

Tears spill out of my eyes.

"Because you fucking own me, Sarah."

He kisses my wet cheeks. He peppers my entire face with soft kisses. He kisses my mouth. I kiss him back. He presses his body into mine. His lips find my eyelids, my ears, my neck. His hands are on my butt, cradling my back, stroking through my hair.

"I thought I lost you tonight," he whispers.

"You almost did."

His breathing halts. "Don't leave me, Sarah." His kiss is full of passion. "Be patient with me," he mumbles into my lips. "I'm doing my best."

I reach under his T-shirt and touch his warm skin. It's sticky with his dried sweat. The muscles over his ribcage ripple under my fingers.

"I know, baby, I know." His kiss is heavenly. "You're doing so good, baby. So, so good," I whisper into his lips.

"Don't leave me."

My body melts into his. "No more secrets, Jonas."

"I promise," he says. He leans back and looks me right in the face. "I'll jump off any waterfall you want, baby. Just don't give up on me."

A light rain begins peppering our faces and splattering softly onto the sidewalk all around us. Oh, Seattle. You're so predictable.

I nod. "Let's go home," I say. "I just figured out another item for my *addendum*."

His eyes light up.

"You're gonna take a flying-squirrel leap off a waterfall for me tonight, baby—whether you like it or not."

Chapter 17
Jonas

Josh looks up from the TV when we burst through the front door, slightly damp from the rain and revved up like two dogs in heat. He's sitting on the couch, watching basketball and drinking a beer.

"Well, well, well. Aren't you the sneaky one, Little Miss Sarah Cruz? So much for me keeping an eye on you tonight. Sorry, bro, she just slipped out without me realizing it."

"I went to spy on Jonas having a drink with a hooker," Sarah says.

"Ah, so you figured out Jonas' brilliant plan, huh?"

"It wasn't hard."

"And did it piss you off?" Josh asks.

"Oh, just a tad," she says.

"Gosh, Jonas. Too bad someone smarter than you didn't warn you about that very thing."

"Yes, I'm a dumbshit, I know," I say. "You should have seen her. She marched in there, kicked ass, and took charge of the whole thing. She was brilliant."

"Why doesn't that surprise me? I seem to recall suggesting you ask her for her input in the first place."

Sarah laughs. "You should have seen Jonas' face when I first walked in. If I'd blown on him, he would have tipped over." She looks at me sideways, her eyes mischievous. "I liked it."

Oh my God, I've got to get this gorgeous woman into my bed.

"Josh, I'm sorry, man, but you've got to get the fuck out of here tonight. Go to a hotel, whatever," I say. I'm losing my mind. My baby's got something sexy up her sleeve and I can't wait to find out what it is. Whatever it is, it's guaranteed to involve her shrieking like a howler monkey tonight and I don't want Josh sitting out here on the couch eating fucking Doritos while she does.

"A hotel?" He looks at the two of us and instantly understands why I'm kicking him out. "Oh come on, man. I'll just go to my room. It's way in the back. I'll listen to music. I'll put a pillow over my head. Come on. I just want to chill tonight and watch the game. I had a long day."

"No, you gotta get the fuck out. Sorry."

He rolls his eyes. "Fine," he huffs. "Maybe I'll give Party Girl with a Hyphen a call." He looks at Sarah. "Can you text me Kat's number?"

"Yeah, sure, but she's busy tonight. She's hanging out with her new bodyguard. Oh, yeah, that reminds me, Jonas, she asked me to thank you profusely. She says her bodyguard's a total hunk—even cuter than Kevin Costner. And she did quite the Whitney Houston impression for me when I called, too."

I laugh.

"You sent her a *bodyguard*?" Josh asks, incredulous. "Why didn't you just ask me? I would have hung out with her and kept her safe and sound."

I shrug. "It didn't even occur to me. Plus, you've got plenty to do, right?" I beam at Sarah. "And, anyway, after Sarah's magnificent performance tonight, I don't feel all that worried about Kat's safety anymore." I kiss Sarah's nose. "You're so fucking smart, baby." I kiss her mouth. She receives me with enthusiasm. Oh God, how I'm going to fuck this woman tonight. First off, I'm going to make love to My Magnificent Sarah with supreme devotion and expertly calibrated skill—and then I'm going to fuck Orgasma the All-Powerful's brains out yet again 'til she comes like a motherfucker.

Josh clears his throat. "I'm still right here."

I pull away from Sarah and glare at Josh. "Don't you have an acquisition report to analyze?" I laugh. I'm such a hypocrite. I haven't put in an honest day's work since we closed the deal on our rock climbing gyms.

"Yeah, actually, I wanted to talk to you about that for a minute," Josh says. "Sarah, do you mind if I steal Jonas for five minutes?"

"Not right now, Josh," I say quickly. "Sarah's gonna make me jump off a waterfall tonight to prove my unwavering devotion to her."

Sarah swats me on the shoulder. "Jonas!"

"What?" I laugh. I look at Josh. "Let's talk tomorrow."

I grab Sarah's hand and pull her toward my room.

"No, I really need to talk to you tonight, bro. Five minutes."

Sarah drops my hand. "Talk to your brother. I need a few minutes to set up the *waterfall*, anyway." She grins broadly and leans into my ear. "I'll be waiting for you, big boy." She smiles at Josh. "Will I see you tomorrow?"

"Probably not." Josh looks at me, stone-faced. Oh shit. Something's up. "But I'll be back in Seattle again soon, no doubt. I'm up here all the time."

She crosses the room to give him a hug. She whispers something to him and he nods. He kisses the top of her head like she's a little kid and she blushes, nodding. She walks out of the room, but not before flashing me a look that makes me grin from ear to ear.

I sit down next to Josh on the couch. "What's up?"

"I was just about to ask you the same thing."

I sigh. I know exactly what he's referring to. "I know. I've been MIA lately. I'm sorry."

"Just tell me straight. What's the deal?"

I let out a long exhale and rub my face. "I can't do it, Josh. Something's clicked inside me and I can't pretend anymore—about anything. I just can't put on a suit and a fucking mask and try to be someone I'm not. I've never been that guy. I can't keep trying to be him. I'm done."

He exhales. "Are you sure?"

"I never gave a shit about Faraday & Sons; you know that. And now that we've got the gyms, and I've got Sarah, I don't have the stomach for bullshit of any variety anymore. I know what I want."

"Yeah? And what's that?"

"Well, thank you for asking. I want to build Climb and Conquer into a worldwide brand. Not just the physical gyms themselves, but an entire lifestyle brand—clothes, shoes, gear, equipment. Maybe even a blog or magazine. The Climb and Conquer brand will embody adventure, fitness, the pursuit of excellence—each person's individual but universal quest to find the divine original form of himself."

Josh smiles. "Sounds pretty awesome, bro."

"This is what I'm meant to do. I don't care about acquiring shit just to acquire more shit. I've already got more money than I know what to do with. What's the fucking point?"

Josh nods. "Okay. What else?"

"I want to climb. Obviously."

Josh nods. This he already knows.

"All over the world. The highest peaks. With you."

"The Two Musketeers."

"Fuck yeah. The Faraday twins."

He half-smiles at me.

"I've had enough of bankers and financial analysts and fucking lawyers and accountants to last a lifetime. I want to be with people who understand me—people who love to climb."

Josh nods. This part he knows, too. I've never really belonged in the high finance world of Faraday & Sons. You wouldn't know it from the outside—you'd assume quite the opposite from the outside, probably, just because I happen to be good at it—but most of the time, secretly, I'm a fish out of water in that world. Josh knows this about me. He's always known. But no one else does. And I don't want to pretend anymore.

I sigh. "And last but certainly not least I want to be with Sarah as much as humanly possible." A shiver runs down my spine. "I almost screwed everything up tonight, Josh. For a minute there, I thought I'd lost her." I run my hand through my hair. "You were right—things weren't nearly as 'simple' as I thought they'd be."

"Surprise, surprise. Yet another flash of brilliance brought to you by Mr. Book Smarts, Jonas Faraday. I told you so, moron."

I shake my head. "I'm not even gonna say fuck you. That's how right you were."

"Thank you for the much-deserved validation. How can a guy be so fucking smart and yet so fucking stupid?"

"I thought she was gonna leave me. And it scared the shit out of me." I swallow hard.

Josh grins at me. "I told you not to fuck it up, and what did you go and do?"

"Almost fucked it up. If it had been any other girl, I'd be toast right now. I got lucky this time, only because she's so smart. But I can't fuck it up like that again or I might not be so lucky next time."

Josh laughs. "She's good for you, bro. I like her."

"I like her, too."

Josh takes a deep breath. "So is that everything you want? Or is there more on the list?"

"One more thing." I bite my lip, trying to decide how to word this. "I'd really like to pull my head out of my ass and give a shit about something bigger than myself." I pause. I haven't thought this one through very well yet. "Maybe Climb and Conquer could adopt some causes and donate a portion of all proceeds—not for some gimmicky promotion, not to get publicity, but as our basic business model. We can talk about which causes we care most about—I've already got a couple in mind, maybe you've got some, too—but the basic idea is that I'd like to actively and unabashedly try to make the world a better a place, every single day."

Josh tilts his head and looks at me like aliens have overtaken my body. And I understand why. I've never said anything like this before. Ever. Between the two of us, despite Josh's love of fast cars and other assorted high-priced toys, he's the one who's more accustomed to wearing a red cape. He's the one who invites little leaguers or kids with leukemia into our box seats at sports games. He's the one who calls his celebrity friends to ask them to donate a signed jersey or guitar to a charity auction. He's the guy a hundred different people would call first if they were to find themselves in a Tijuana prison or on a desolate highway with no gas in their tank. And, of course, he's the one who's picked me up every time I've fallen down.

I'm suddenly thinking about Sarah—how passionate she is about wanting to help people and make the world a better place. How she puts her money where her mouth is every single day. Josh and I have all the money in the world, but what do we do with it? And then there's Sarah who comes from nothing and is working her ass off to get a full-ride scholarship, just so she can take a job after graduation that pays next to nothing, all so she can help others. My heart's suddenly in my throat. She makes me want to be a better man.

"I'm gonna start being the guy I should have been all along," I say quietly. "The divine original form of Jonas Faraday." I exhale. "The man she would have wanted me to become."

Josh's eyes are moist. He rubs them. He knows exactly who the "she" is in that sentence. He clears his throat, but he's unable to speak.

There's a long beat. The rain outside has gathered strength. It's beating loudly against the windows and the roof.

Josh slaps his face, hard. "Okay, crazy-ass motherfucker. Sounds like a fucking plan."

I slap mine in reply. "Okay, pussy-ass-bitch-motherfucker."

"I'm proud of you, Jonas," Josh says quietly.

"I'm proud of you, too."

We look at each other for a brief moment. The Faraday boys weren't raised to say "I love you" to each other—or to anyone, for that matter—quite the opposite—but Josh and I have just said it to each other in our own way.

"When do you wanna put out a press release about your departure?" Josh asks.

"Give me a couple days at least. I'll write it personally so it doesn't leak before release. And I want to be the one who tells Uncle William, of course—I owe him that much. Plus, I've got to tell my team. I want to assure them their jobs are secure, that we'll keep the team intact, continue pushing forward with acquisitions, blah, blah, fucking blah. And we'll have to put some thought into who should take over managing my team, whether we want to look internally or put out a nationwide search. Or, I guess, you could just assume management of my team along with yours. That would probably make the most sense—you come up to Seattle so much, anyway."

Josh is stone-faced. He doesn't speak.

"What do you think?"

Josh doesn't reply.

"Josh? Any thoughts?"

He exhales loudly. "Shit, man. I don't give a fuck about Faraday & Sons, either."

Chapter 18
Sarah

I expect Jonas to feel apprehensive at first, or maybe even anxious, given the forcible bondage of his mother he witnessed as a boy—and that's exactly why I chose this activity as his metaphorical waterfall in the first place. My actual waterfall in Belize was thirty feet tall, after all, so his symbolic waterfall can't be a frickin' pony ride. I'm just hoping that, with a little bit of coaxing and tenderness, or, as the case may be, a little tough love, he'll be able to view this situation through new eyes—his *adult* eyes—and perhaps replace some of the tortured memories from his childhood with new, delectable, decidedly adult (and pleasurable) memories. Hey, it's worth a shot.

Jonas' bed frame is a sleek design without bedposts, so I need to get creative. I improvise four long tethers using neckties from Jonas' closet and loop them around the base of each leg of his bed. I finish off this brilliant feat of modern engineering with a dandy slipknot at the end of each tether (courtesy of a handy "how to" video on YouTube). The whole setup isn't nearly as simple or functional as the luxurious bondage sheet with soft Velcro cuffs described in reverent detail in one of the applications I reviewed, but, hey, my Jonas-Shall-Surrender-to-Me-and-Thusly-Expunge-the-Remainder-of-His-Demons idea only came to me an hour ago. I think I've improvised pretty well considering the timeframe and what I've got on hand.

I venture into Jonas' closet in search of variously textured items I might be able to tease and tantalize him with during his captivity, but there's not much to choose from. His closet is filled with meticulously hung suits and shirts, perfectly-folded jeans and T-shirts, immaculately lined-up shoes, and an assortment of the latest in athletic clothes, fleeces and jackets. It's quintessential Jonas—simple, well ordered, and beautiful—and absolutely nothing of any use to a dirty little minx like me. The man doesn't seem to own anything even remotely feathered or furry or beaded or fringed—and, hey, no big surprise, there aren't any whips, chains, nipple clamps, butt plugs, dildos, or horse bits, either (thankfully). I smile. My hunky-monkey boyfriend is a man of simple tastes. I like that about him. Even if the Sex Factory were located right next door with an unlimited supply of toys to choose from, I wouldn't want any of it, at least not tonight. First off, I've never used that kind of stuff before and I have no idea how any of it works. But more importantly, that's not what turns Jonas on. As I say, he's a man of simple tastes. And this whole exercise is about turning Jonas on—and forcing him to succumb to a new kind of trust with me.

I take a quick shower and brush my teeth and then crawl onto the bed to await Jonas. I put my fancy new laptop next to me and turn on "Sweater Weather" by The Neighbourhood. I love this song. I close my eyes and stretch myself out, breathing deeply and letting the song wash over me. I begin touching myself, letting images from my dream revisit me—ten poltergeist-Jonases pleasuring me simultaneously. Warm red wine gushing across my belly and spilling into my crotch and down my thighs and between my toes, and Jonas licking the wine off every inch of me. A room full of people watching us. By the time I get to Jonas proclaiming, "I love Sarah Cruz," loud enough for our entire audience to hear, I'm highly aroused and aching for him.

The bedroom door finally opens.

I look up at him, licking my lips with anticipation.

He takes in the web of neckties tethered to the legs of his bed and his face falls.

"No, Sarah," he says simply.

Exactly the reaction I expected. He was unequivocal in his application that bondage of any kind is a non-starter for him. "Non-negotiable," he called it. But that was before he met me. Before I jumped off a waterfall in a dark cave for him. Before we became mutually stricken with a serious mental disease. Before I became Orgasma the All-Powerful. Before he checked in with Stacy the Faker behind my back and made me doubt him.

"Yes," I purr. "Come here, baby."

"Not this," he says. "I'm sorry."

I get up off the bed and go to him. I grab his hands and pull him toward the bed.

He resists. He's immovable.

"I've never done this, either. But I want to do it with you."

I begin unbuttoning his jeans.

He takes a step back. "I won't tie you up, Sarah. Absolutely not."

I smile. "Oh, baby, no. *You're* not gonna tie *me* up. *I'm* gonna tie *you* up."

He inhales sharply. That's not what he was expecting me to say. His face turns pale.

I step toward him again. I touch his lips, his beautifully sculpted lips. "I allegedly own you? Well, tonight, you're going to prove it."

His chest heaves.

"Do you trust me?"

He closes his eyes. "Ask me to do anything else for you. Just not this."

"Trust me," I say. "Come on."

He sighs. "I have no interest in this, Sarah."

"I had no interest in jumping off a thirty-foot waterfall into ink-black water in a darkened cave. But you gave me no choice—and it changed my life. I'm not giving you a choice, either. This is your waterfall."

He lets out a long, controlled exhale.

"Jonas, contrary to my every instinct, I jumped—literally and figuratively. And my body thanked me for it later. And so did my soul. Well, now it's your turn."

He shifts his weight. He shakes his head.

My ire rises. "It's your penance for what you pulled tonight." This is my trump card. "As far as I'm concerned, you've got no other way down."

His gaze is defiant. "'Knowledge which is acquired under compulsion obtains no hold on the mind.'"

He doesn't need to tell me that's yet another quote from frickin' Plato. Screw Plato. "I've got a Plato quote for you, too," I say. "I looked it up, just for you."

He squints at me.

"'Courage is a kind of salvation.'"

He scowls.

"Come on, baby," I say softly. "Madness. Detach your mind from your body. You'll thank me."

He looks over at the bed. "Sarah . . ."

"Madness," I repeat.

He pauses for a long beat and finally takes off his shirt. His muscled chest rises and falls with each anxious breath.

I take in the glorious sight of him—man, oh man, I'll never tire of looking at him with his shirt off. I touch the tattoo on his left forearm. "For a man to conquer himself is the first and noblest of all victories," I whisper, quoting his own tattoo back to him.

He nods.

I pull at the waist of his jeans and he takes them off.

He stands before me naked, his erection defying whatever misgivings his brain might be having.

I look him up and down. He's spectacular. The sight of him never gets old. Day-am.

"Lemme take a quick shower," he says. He swallows hard.

"Hurry."

He's gone.

I crawl back onto the bed, cue up another song on my laptop ("Fall In Love" by Phantogram), and wait—losing myself in my dream again. Wine, poltergeist-Jonases, licking, fucking, spectators. *I love Sarah Cruz.* The throbbing between my legs is excruciating.

I feel his warm skin against mine. His lips on my breast. His hand on the inside of my thigh, creeping up.

"No," I whisper. "I'm in charge this time."

"Let me make love to you," he whispers, his lips trailing down my belly.

I'm tempted to give in, to let go and let him pleasure me all night long.

But holy hell. I put a lot of effort into this bondage setup, and, by God, I'm going to use it. I sit up and push him back. "You do as I command. You're no longer allowed the luxury of free will from this moment forward."

He smashes his lips together.

"I'm serious."

His eyes move from my face down to my naked body. "You look beautiful," he whispers. His erection twitches. "Can't we just make love?"

"Jonas, I just said you've got no free will. Don't speak unless spoken to."

"I can't help it. You're too beautiful. Mesmerizing. You're the goddess and the muse, Sarah Cruz."

I ignore him and scoot off the bed. "Come here."

He rolls his eyes but reluctantly rolls off the side of the bed to join me. He comes to a hulking stand in front of me, his erection straining for me, his muscles tensing in all their glory.

"From here on out, don't speak unless spoken to. My will shall be done."

He sighs.

"If you wig out or something, I'll stop and untie you. Just say... um..." I stop. I've never done this before. Jeez, I'm a terrible dominatrix.

"You're trying to come up with a 'safe word'?" he asks, incredulous.

"Yeah. A safe word." My finger traces a deep ridge in his abs, just above his erect penis. The throbbing between my legs intensifies.

His breathing hitches when I touch him. "Sarah, come on. Just let me taste you. I'm gonna make you shriek like a howler monkey, and then I'm gonna fuck your brains out and make you come again." His fingers lightly graze my breast. "Come on."

I swat his hand away. "I can't stand here buck naked looking at you anymore, Jonas. You're too beautiful. I'm gonna start dripping down my thigh. Are you gonna get on the bed and let me tie you up or what?"

"Sarah," he sighs. "I don't do bondage. You don't understand. I can't."

"You *think* you can't, but you can—with me, you can. With me, anything is possible."

He grunts with frustration. "You don't understand."

I'm getting testy. "You owe me one goddamned waterfall, Jonas Faraday. *One waterfall,* that's all I ask." I cross my arms. "This shouldn't be that hard. Any other man would be leaping onto the bed right now with glee. *Juepucha, culo.*"

He opens his mouth to say something, but closes it again. He shifts his weight. He exhales. "If I do this, it's gonna be just this once. And then we're done with bondage bullshit forever."

I'm noncommittal. We'll see.

"Sarah, you don't understand why this is a hot button for me." He rubs his eyes. "Fuck."

The hairs on the back of my neck stand up. Maybe this wasn't such a good idea. "What? Tell me," I say. I'm suddenly unsure.

"Never mind." His jaw is clenched. "I'll do it." He marches over to the bed and sits, his erection belying his internal struggle. "Let's do it."

"Jonas?"

"It's fine," he says. "You want proof you own me, here it is. Let's go. Tie me up and do what you want to me."

I pause, assessing him. This isn't how I envisioned this going. I thought he'd be apprehensive, sure, but he seems downright pissed. "Okay," I finally say slowly, not sure how to navigate this situation. "So what's the safe word?"

"I'm not gonna need a fucking safe word. What could you possibly do to me that I'd need a safe word?"

"We're supposed to have one."

"Who says?"

I throw up my hands. "I don't know—blogs. I've never done this before." I shake my head. "So you're gonna fight me every step of the way? For the love of Pete, you are the worst submissive, ever. You're totally ruining this whole fantasy for me right now. Damn, I was so turned on, too."

He glares at me. "Fine," he concedes, but his eyes remain hard. "We'll have a safe word." He looks up at the ceiling, thinking.

"Plato?"

That brings out a half-smile. His eyes soften. "Fuck no. Don't bring fucking Plato into our bed of bondage. Jesus. Have some respect for the forefather of modern philosophical thought."

I smile at him. "Okay. How about we keep it simple, then. Stop?"

"No. I always tell you to stop when you hijack me, but I never mean it. I can't resist you, you know that." He motions to one of the tethers on the bed. "Case in point."

"Fine. You pick it, then. It can be anything. Cat, dog, watermelon, Pixie Stix, Dumbledore, whatever."

His smile broadens, despite himself. "I really don't think it's necessary." He has a sudden thought. "You're not planning to actually *hurt* me, right? Not for real?"

"Of course, not. I don't fantasize about pain any more than you do. I'm just gonna, you know, get my rocks off by getting you off."

"You're gonna get your rocks off? Who says that? You're so adorable, I swear to God."

"Jonas, this is not going the way I envisioned it at all." I sit next to him on the bed. "I'm trying to bring you to your knees here, make you surrender to me, drive you crazy. And you're not cooperating at all." I pout.

"Baby," he says, putting his arms around me. "Just let me lick your sweet pussy and make you come and I promise on all things holy I'll surrender to you. You're my goddess—I don't need a fucking necktie around my wrist to prove it. Come on, baby." He brushes his hand between my legs. "Your pussy is calling to me like a siren. I can almost taste it now." He gently dips his finger into me and brings his wet finger to his mouth. "Mmm."

I shudder with arousal.

"Let me make up for what I did tonight by getting you off like a freight train." His hand brushes between my legs and his tongue licks my neck. "You're so ready for me, baby, holy shit." His mouth moves to my mine.

I summon every bit of willpower in my body and pull away from him. I stand.

"Goddamnit, Jonas, this whole relationship isn't about what *you* want. Sometimes, it's about what *I* want, too." I feel heat rising in my cheeks. "And I want this."

He's incredulous. "All I ever think about is what you want. Your pleasure is mine. Always." He stands, his face earnest.

"Well, this is the pleasure I want. Just this once." I jut my chin at him. "You lured me up a waterfall with only one way down. So that's what I'm doing to you. This is your waterfall. Are you gonna jump or not?" My crotch is on fire. I'm not going to be able to hold out much longer without saying to hell with it and jumping his bones.

He sighs. "Yes, I'm gonna jump. You know I am. I can't resist you."

"Okay, then. Let's figure out our safe word already. Jeez." I grab my phone off the nightstand and sit down on the edge of the bed again. He sits next to me, looking over my shoulder at the screen. A Google search of "What is a good safe word?" yields instantaneous results. "Oh, brother," I say, shaking my head. "The trusty 'green, yellow, red system.' That's not obvious or anything."

"Ah," Jonas nods. "People are so clever, aren't they?"

I toss my phone onto the nightstand. "Okay, so green is 'full steam ahead.' Yellow is 'I'm not thrilled but don't stop yet.' Red is 'Stop right now, you fucking freak, I'm totally wigging out.'"

He laughs. "You sound like a pro already." He looks around the room with mock concern. "You don't have a big bag of dildos lying around here, do you? This is just gonna be me and you, right—no foreign objects?"

I smirk. "You'll just have to wait and see. You never know what I might do to you."

"Seriously?" He looks genuinely wary.

I roll my eyes. "Jonas, no, not seriously. I'm not gonna shove a giant dildo up your ass or burn you with cigarettes or pee on you. Just lie down on the bed and trust me. Any time you want me to stop, just say red and I will, I promise." I look at him expectantly. "But after I get started, I guarantee you won't want me to stop." I smile.

He sighs. "Sex should be about pleasure. Nothing else. Not pain."

"Duh, Jonas. Big, fat duh. Have some faith, for the love of Pete. Your pleasure is mine, baby. This is all about pleasure—*your* pleasure. This is just gonna be you and me."

He exhales, yet again. "Okay." He scoots to the middle of the bed. "For you."

"Thank you, Baby Jesus!" I raise my hands to the heavens in gratitude. "Okay, starting now, I'm in charge."

"Just be kind, baby. That's all I ask."

"I know of no other way."

Chapter 19
Jonas

"Too tight?" she asks.

I pull on the restraints. "No."

I can't believe I'm letting her do this to me. If she only knew about the last time I was restrained like this, albeit under completely different circumstances, she'd never ask this of me. Fuck. She's the only person I'd ever let do this to me. Fuck. I never should have said yes.

"Are you comfortable?"

"No."

"Let me rephrase. Do you need an adjustment to your physical environment in any way?"

"No."

"You're a terrible submissive, you know that?"

I sigh. "I should hope so."

She pulls out yet another necktie and places it over my eyes.

"No, baby. Please. Seeing you is what turns me on. Your skin. Your eyes. Your hair. Please."

"Shh," she says. "No more talking."

The song on her laptop ends and the sound of rain pelting the windowpane bleeds into the room.

She secures the blindfold. I can't see a fucking thing. I bite my lip. My heart pounds in my chest. My stomach twists. I feel sick. And yet my dick is rock hard. Go figure.

"Yellow," I whisper.

"I haven't even done anything to you yet."

"Just... the whole thing. Sarah, listen."

There's silence.

"I'm listening," she says softly.

I pause. The rain has gathered strength outside the window. "Never mind."

I can't tell her about The Lunacy. Not now, not like this. She knows I'm fucked up, yes, but she doesn't know I'm *that* fucked up. She wouldn't want me if she knew.

"Did Josh leave?" she asks.

"Please don't mention my brother at a time like this—you're gonna make me puke."

"I need to get something from the kitchen and I'm naked, you big dummy."

"Oh my, aren't you the sassy little dominatrix now? Yeah. He went to the airport."

"I'll be right back."

She's gone. I'm alone with the sound of the rain. Why did I let her to do this to me? I'm fucking blindfolded and spread-eagle with a raging hard-on, trussed up like a calf at a rodeo. There is no other woman I'd do this for in the entire galaxy.

She returns. She places something on the nightstand. Sounds like a cup. Or cups. Something rattling around? Ice cubes in a glass.

Music begins playing. The song is "Magic" by Coldplay. Good song. Surely, she's chosen it to send a lyrical message to me.

"Yellow," I whisper, sending a lyrical message right back to her. I'll see her one Coldplay song and raise her another—my favorite one, in fact—the one in which Chris Martin of Coldplay offers up his very lifeblood to the woman he loves. I'd give my blood to Sarah, too, all of it, every last drop—or, as it turns out, let her tie me up. For me, they're one and the same thing.

"Don't use one of the safe words unless you're serious. No crying wolf." There's a beat. "Wait, are you serious?"

"No, I was just commenting on your choice of Coldplay songs— remarking on the one I'd play for you if I were in charge." Oh, how I wish I were untied right now and making love to her to "Yellow." That song would tell her I love her in the way my own mouth can't— and my body would emphatically prove it.

"Jonas." She's annoyed with me. "No talking. And no Boy Who Cried Wolf with the safe words. As your dominatrix, I have to honor the safe words unflinchingly—I take my vows very seriously."

"Your vows?"

"My dominatrix vows."

I can't help but laugh, even in this situation. Sarah can always make me laugh.

"Okay, Mistress, proceed," I say. "I shouldn't have interrupted your brilliant strategy."

"Based on your gigantic hard-on, it doesn't appear you mind my brilliant strategy all that much."

"My dick has a mind of its own. Pay no attention to the man behind the curtain."

She kisses me. "Seriously, are you okay?"

"Will you just take off the blindfold, please? It's making me claustrophobic."

She sighs. "The blog I read says what I'm about to do is most effective when you're blindfolded—it enhances the sensation."

Her voice is so earnest. I can't resist her. "Fine. Do what you will, Mistress. You own me."

She kisses my lips and giggles.

I instinctively reach for her and the restraints tighten around my wrists. My chest constricts. Talk about sense memory. Déjà fucking vu. My mind hurtles back to that night when they first had me tied up like fucking King Kong. A virtual army of orderlies, or whoever the fuck they were, bum rushed me when I started flipping out. They pumped me with so many drugs after that, I don't remember every detail clearly—but I sure as hell remember the restraints around my wrists and ankles—the ones that felt exactly like these—and how I begged and pleaded with them to untie me so I could put an end to my lifelong misery once and for all. For weeks, my wrists bore deep bruises from how violently I'd thrashed against my restraints during that first horrible night of The Lunacy.

The lyrics to "Yellow" float through my mind. Just like the song says, I'd give her every last drop of blood in my body.

Her soft lips are on my neck, my nipples, trailing down to my stomach.

I reach for her and the restraints pull on me again. I inhale deeply, trying to calm myself, but the ties around my wrists keep pulling me back to the dark movie playing inside my head—to the night my mind finally, painfully succumbed to a decade's worth of torment.

An ice cube on my nipple jerks me back to the present. She swirls it around and across my chest and then down to my abs, her warm wet tongue trailing immediately behind the icy wetness like some kind of erotic Zamboni. Soft skin brushes against my erection— her nipple?—as her lips meander their way down my torso. I shudder.

I want to touch her. I need to touch her. I reach out to her yet again and the restraints tug forcefully on my wrists. My stomach twists.

Even as I climbed the stairs after hearing the gunshot coming from his room, I knew whatever awaited me would push my mind over the edge and into the dark abyss. And yet I continued climbing those fucking stairs, one brutal step at a time, slowly, involuntarily, inevitably, to my doom—his room a monstrous magnet and my body a passive slab of steel.

I'd give her every last drop of blood in my body.

"Yellow," I whisper.

"What part? The ice?"

"No. The blindfold. Take it off. Please." My words choke in my throat. I'm dangerously close to thrashing around, but I breathe deeply and control myself.

Her hands touch my face. She removes the blindfold. Her face is awash in disappointment. "I'm sorry," she says. "I just wanted to try something."

I'm being a total pussy-ass right now. She looks so sad. I sigh. "It's okay, baby. Put it back on. Do your thing. I'm sorry."

"No, it's okay. No blindfold. Just keep your eyes closed, okay?"

"Okay."

"Promise?"

"Yes."

"Swear?"

"Yep."

She throws the blindfold onto the floor and I close my eyes.

I feel her rolling to the side of the bed. The song stops.

A new song comes on. Holy fucking Christ, no, no, no—it's fucking One Direction, "What Makes You Beautiful." Just shoot me now and send me to hell with my father where I fucking belong.

My eyes spring open. "No," I shout. "A fate worse than death."

She glares at me. "Close your eyes. You swore."

151

I comply.

Her lips are in my ear. "This song is intended to punish you for your despicable actions earlier this evening." Her tone is low and even. "You were a very, very bad boy. You lied to me through omission. You didn't trust me. And that opened the door for me to mistrust you—not a good foundation for a healthy relationship, Jonas. And now I'm going to suck your cock to the dulcet sounds of One Direction to teach you a lesson. And as further punishment, from this day forward, whenever you hear this song in a passing car or in a grocery store, you'll instantly get rock hard, remembering what I did to you tonight."

Well, that shuts me the fuck up—along with the voices inside my head, too. All of us—me, myself, and I—instantly give this woman our undivided attention.

She chuckles, clearly amused by herself, and moves away from my ear.

The abominable song blares at me, making my head hurt and my ears bleed. It's a travesty is what it is—a fucking crime against humanity. But then her tongue licks my cock like it's a melting ice cream cone and I don't give a fuck what song is playing. When she takes me into her mouth, it's really, really warm in there—and extra wet—holy fuck, she's got warm liquid in her mouth that she's swirling around my cock, like she's treating it to its own personal Jacuzzi.

I let out a low moan. I wish I could look at her right now, but a promise is a promise.

Her mouth leaves me.

I instinctively reach my hand toward her, willing her to return to me, needing to touch her, and the restraint stops me. Motherfucker.

I'd give her every last drop of blood in my body, if she wanted me to.

When I first beheld the horror he so meticulously staged for me, I gripped my sanity with all my white-knuckled might, determined not to let go of it—determined not to let him win. If only I'd turned around right then and marched out the door, if only I'd turned my back on him and his malice and his hatred and his decade's worth of blame, if only I'd refused to let him have the last word just that one time, maybe I would have been able to hang onto my mind against all odds, even amid that final, horrific opera he'd performed just for me.

But, no, I didn't turn my back on him and I didn't leave the room and I therefore didn't save myself. Instead, I did the worst thing I could have done. I saw the envelope on his desk, his blood splattered across the neat lettering of my name, and I opened it. Even as I did it, I knew opening that envelope would be my last sane act, I fucking knew it—I knew my mind wouldn't be able to withstand his final parting shot to me any more than his brain had withstood the final parting shot from his shotgun—but I opened it anyway.

She takes my cock into her mouth again, but this time her mouth is icy cold wetness. The intense sensation jerks me out of the horror show in my head and puts me back in the room with Sarah. Surprisingly, the change in temperature feels exhilarating—acutely pleasurable. *My Magnificent Sarah.*

The sound that comes out of me is primal.

"You like that?" she asks. Her voice is gravelly and thick with arousal.

"Yes," I say.

For a few blissful moments, her oh so talented mouth makes me forget all about my restraints. Just as I'm about to lose control and release into her mouth, her mouth leaves my cock, her hand grips my shaft, and her naked body writhes against mine.

"I don't want you to come," she says, panting, her lips touching my ear. "Your job is to stay hard for me. You understand?"

"Yes," I choke out.

"If you're in danger of coming, you're required to tell me so. You can say 'I'm gonna come' all you like, but if you really are gonna cross the line, you'll say 'limit' so I know."

I nod.

I hear the sound of movement at the nightstand.

I shiver with anticipation.

Her face is next to mine again. I smell the unmistakable scent of Altoids mints. Her tongue laps at my lips for one tantalizing second. "I'm going to make your cock feel minty fresh," she says. Her voice is husky.

She takes me into her mouth again. And damn, yes, minty fresh is right.

I'd give anything to see her brown eyes looking up at me from down there, but, fuck me, I promised to keep my eyes closed. I try to imagine what she must look like right now—try to imagine her big brown eyes blazing up at me—but the thought is such a turn on, I have to stop thinking about it or else I'll come like a motherfucker into her mouth. She sucks on my tip gently with just the right amount of pressure and I jerk violently.

"Limit." Holy fuck. "Limit."

Her mouth leaves my cock and finds my belly button. Her lips are warm.

She's moaning, shuddering. This is turning her on as much as me. She crawls on top of me and places my tip at her wet entrance. I jerk my pelvis up, trying to enter her, but she tilts away. I'm a caged lion swatting at a hunk of raw meat that's being pulled on a string just out of my reach. And all the while, that fucking One Direction song tortures me.

I want to reach out and touch her hair. I want to touch her sweet wet pussy and make her come. I want to hold her, cradle her, lick her, fuck her without mercy. I want to make her scream my name.

One Direction, thankfully, stops.

"You can open your eyes now." Her voice is dripping with her arousal.

I open my eyes. Oh God, I could come at the mere sight of her if I let myself. Her cheeks are flushed. Her eyes are wild. A sheen of perspiration covers her face. She's in ecstasy and I haven't even touched her. She's beautiful.

"Limit," I whisper, looking into her eyes.

She moves to put on another song. "Do I Wanna Know?" by the Arctic Monkeys. Yet another reason to love this woman.

She straddles my lap, teasing me yet again, writhing, and bends over to kiss my mouth.

"You're going to lick me now," she says.

"Untie me."

"No."

"Untie me."

"Just give it a chance. Trust me." She flashes her most seductive smile.

"I'm not going to lick your pussy with these restraints on. You're my religion and licking your pussy is going to church."

She doesn't understand. "Trust me, Jonas."

"Red."

She opens her mouth, shocked.

"Red," I say again.

Her shoulders slump.

"You want me to inhabit heaven and hell at the same time. It's not possible. I choose heaven."

Her face droops.

She silently unties my wrists, defeated.

I rub my wrists and sit up to untie my ankles.

When I'm freed of my restraints, I lie back down on the bed in the same exact position I was in a moment ago—my arms outstretched, my legs spread-eagle.

I'm giving her my blood.

"I'm a free man now, baby—and your slave by choice. Do whatever you were about to do and I won't move a muscle. You own me."

She pouts. "Obviously not."

"Come on, baby, my devotion binds me ten times more fiercely than any physical restraint ever could."

She continues pouting.

"I'm in the same position I was in when forcibly bound—but now I'm willingly bound. I'm your voluntary slave. Come on. You own me."

She doesn't move. The look on her face grabs my heart and squeezes it.

"Green," I whisper softly. "Come on."

She looks crestfallen.

"Green, green, green," I say. "Green?"

Her eyes perk up a little bit.

"Green, green, green, green, green, green, green. Full steam ahead. I'm at your mercy, pretty baby."

Her mouth twists into a half-smile, but she doesn't move.

"Come on, baby. You're my religion. Licking your pussy is going to church. And your name's my sacred prayer. *Sarah.*"

Her eyes ignite.

"Green," I whisper. "Come on, pretty baby."

She nods.

She maneuvers her body up to my face and places her knees on either side of my head. Slowly, delicately, she lowers herself onto me and sits on my face. With a loud and grateful groan, I begin licking her. Oh thank you, Lord in heaven above, yes, I lick her. Halle-fucking-lujah. It takes every ounce of self-restraint not to grab her ass, but I stay true to my word and keep my arms out to my sides like I'm on the cross. And, in a sense, I suppose, I am.

She gyrates and jerks her pelvis, moaning and groaning as she does, her excitement quickly escalating into powerful thrusts and high-pitched shrieks. Just as her entire body begins to shake, she swivels completely around, panting and sweaty, bends over my torso, and takes my cock into her mouth as I continue eating her glorious pussy.

My Magnificent Sarah, hallowed be thy name, thy kingdom come, thy will be done, on earth as it is in heaven. She's a church hymn, howling at the top of her lungs. With one final, insistent shriek, her body ripples and seizes into my tongue. I yank my cock out of her mouth to avoid her soon-to-be clenched jaw.

When I feel her climax ebb and her body go limp, I leap up, growling like a silverback, and toss her onto the bed. In one fluid motion, I bend her compliant body over the edge of the bed, plunge myself into her wetness, and fuck her without mercy until she screams my fucking name. *For thine is the kingdom, the power, and the glory, for ever and ever. Amen.*

Chapter 20
Sarah

He "safe worded" me and then fucked my brains out. What the hell? And now he's gone mute. We're both just lying here in bed together, one blink away from mutual catatonia, not speaking. I look over at him. Yeah, he's awake. I feel like he owes me an explanation. But based on his silence, I guess he disagrees.

Why exactly did he feel the need to use the safe word with me at that particular moment? I realize he's fucked up, and understandably so, given what he witnessed as a boy, but how could he put on the brakes *right then*? True, I can't imagine what kind of crazy he must battle on a daily basis after seeing what he saw, but I wasn't raping him, for Pete's sake—far from it. Even when I had him bound and tethered and at my utter mercy, my only impulse was to give him as much pleasure as I could muster—and not just any kind of pleasure, but the exact pleasure he always says he craves the most. So why on earth did he need the safe word *right then*?

I wanted so badly to give him a special gift tonight—a new kind of bondage memory to replace the one that's tortuously engrained in his gray matter. And, really, childhood trauma or not, would it have killed him to just let me take the driver's seat in our sex life, just this once? Why can't he just trust me and let go? I've had some childhood traumas of my own, thank you very much, but with each magical day and night we've shared, I'm somehow managing to conquer them.

"Hey, have you actually written that report, or were you bluffing?" he finally says.

This is what he wants to talk about right now? The Club? That's the last thing on my mind.

"What do you think?"

"I think you were bluffing."

"You've been with me twenty-four seven from the minute I found out the truth. When the heck would I have had time to write a detailed report? I haven't had time to paint my nails let alone write a report like that." It's not my intention, but that last part came out sounding kinda bitchy.

"Are you mad at me?"

I turn on my side to look at him. "No."

"Because you sound kind of pissed."

I take a deep breath and gather my thoughts. He looks at me expectantly.

"No, I'm not mad. I'm just totally freaking out."

His face turns ashen. "About what?"

"Jonas, I haven't studied in a whole week." Tears well up in my eyes, despite my best efforts to hold them back. "So much is riding on my grades and all I've been doing for a solid week is playing sex kitten with you. I've got to study, Jonas. I've got to focus and get some order back into my life and remember why I went to law school in the first place—" The tears break free and drop out of my eyes. "I've got a lot of people depending on me." Oh God, I'm a hot mess. "And now, thanks to my big mouth, I've got to write a damned *Pelican Brief* as soon as possible, too."

He wraps his arms around me. "Baby, don't you realize there's nothing riding on your grades anymore?" He kisses my cheek and wipes my tears with his thumb.

I pull back to look into his face. I don't understand what he means. The top ten students at the end of the first year get a full-ride scholarship for the next two years, which means students eleven and below are shit out of luck to the tune of some sixty-five thousand dollars. This is my ticket to do whatever I want after graduation, including taking a job that pays peanuts but makes me genuinely happy. We're talking about me trying to win life-changing money here, and all I have to do is study my ass off for one short year of my life. And yet, in the home stretch right before finals, here I am playing sex addict night and day with Jonas. I need to get a grip and refocus my priorities.

He rolls his eyes like I'm a silly little girl. "If you get the scholarship, great. That'll be a fantastic accomplishment and we'll celebrate. But if not, I'll pick up the tab. How much could law school tuition possibly be—fifty grand a year? So we're talking maybe a hundred grand total? No big deal. Just consider yourself the lucky recipient of the Jonas Faraday Scholarship Fund." He beams a huge smile at me.

I can't even believe what I'm hearing. *The lucky recipient?* He expects me to hinge my entire future on his fickle beneficence? On a spur of the moment reassurance made in bed? I'm the *lucky recipient,* he says? Well, I've got news for him—I'm not going to pin my entire future on luck—or on his charity, for that matter.

He smiles at me. "Problem solved. The only thing you have to worry about is passing the bar exam at the end of year three. Between now and then, just go to class and do your best, but don't stress it." He touches my face. "I'm sure we'll figure out something you can do with all your newfound free time."

I stare at him, my mouth agape.

"Okay. What else are you freaking out about? Tee it up and I'll knock it out of the park for you, baby."

I sit up in the bed. I can't even muster a response.

"Come on. Whatever it is, I'll fix it for you."

"You really expect me to let you pay my tuition?"

He shrugs. "Yeah."

"I didn't want to accept a laptop from you and now I'm supposed to accept two years worth of law school tuition?"

He smiles broadly. Apparently, that's a yes.

"And you expect me to just sit back and *chillax* about it, as if you paying my tuition six months from now is some sort of foregone conclusion? Like your pillow talk today is an ironclad promise tomorrow?"

His smile vanishes. The playful sparkle drains from his eyes. "What I'm saying to you isn't pillow talk." Oh man, he's pissed.

"You didn't trust me enough to tell me about Stacy tonight, you won't talk to me about the 'hell' I apparently forced you to endure tonight—your word, not mine—and yet I'm supposed to put my entire future in your hands and just believe on faith that six months from now, come what may between us, you'll still be in the generous mood to write that tuition check for me?" Oh, good Lord, I'm shouting. I can't stop the torrent flowing out of me. "What if you get bored with me between now and then—where would that leave me? What if, God forbid, I push just a little too hard, ask just a little too much of the Emotionally Scarred Adonis and scare you away? Hmm? What then? Would you come back to write my tuition check then?"

He looks like I just stabbed him in the heart. He opens his mouth but closes it again. Oh holy hell. The look in his eyes is unadulterated pain. And yet, for some reason, I blaze right ahead.

"You want me to put every single one of my eggs into the basket of a man who likens his feelings for me to a serious mental disease? To *insanity*? Yeah, that sure makes a girl feel über confident about having a long and secure future with a guy." Holy shit, I can't believe I just said that. Up until this very second, I thought I was perfectly fine with our coded language of love.

His face contorts. He shakes his head, but he doesn't speak. His eyes are moist.

"I'm losing myself, Jonas. I just have to get back to standing on my own two feet."

"Why?"

"Why? *Why*?" I open and close my mouth several times, flummoxed. "Why do I have to breathe? Or eat? It's fundamental."

"No, it's not. You don't *have* to stand on your own two feet. Not all the time. When you can't, or even if you just don't want to sometimes, then I'll carry you. I *want* to carry you."

No one has ever said anything like this to me before. Not even close.

"*Estamos de luna de miel,*" he says softly in his horrible Americano accent. *We're on our honeymoon.* He looks at me hopefully.

For some reason, that phrase doesn't make me swoon the way it did the first time he said it to me.

"Except we're not really, are we?" I spit out. "This could all be over next week and where would that leave me? I can't rely on this and let everything I've worked for slip away."

Oh good Lord, whatever knife I stabbed him with a minute ago, I just turned it.

I soften. "I know I'll never be able to understand what you went through as a child," I say. I inhale and exhale slowly, trying to regain control of my voice. "I'll never be able to fully understand why tonight felt like 'hell' for you—but, Jonas, I *want* to understand." My lip is trembling. "I just wanted to replace your bad childhood memories with good adult ones. I wanted to give you pleasure—to try to heal you. And you wouldn't trust me enough to let me try. I'm tired of everything being the Jonas Faraday Club all the time. I just wanted you to join the Sarah Cruz Club for a change."

"This is all because I wouldn't stay tied up while I ate you out?" He's utterly pained.

"No, Jonas. You're so clueless sometimes. Forget about that. Tonight just made me realize how much you're holding back and I'm not."

"Everyone holds back, sometimes."

"I'm not holding back at all."

"You're not holding back at all?" he asks, incredulous.

"Not at all," I say. And it's true, other than the fact that I have to bite my tongue every five minutes to keep myself from blurting, "I love you!" at the top of my lungs. But that can't be helped.

He stares at me, daring me to confess some deep, dark secret I'm keeping from him—as if he's hoping to prove my fuckeduppedness matches his own.

"Well, okay, one thing," I confess.

His face lights up with anticipatory vindication.

"I secretly like that One Direction song."

He laughs, despite the pained look in his eyes.

"A lot," I add. I put my hands over my face. I can't stop the tears from coming.

"Sarah, what's going on?" He puts his arm around me. "Please, please, don't let this be the part where you say I don't 'let you in.'" His face is awash in anxiety. "Please don't say I'm just too fucked up for you." He's holding back tears.

I touch his beautiful face. "No, Jonas. It's just the opposite. You can never be too fucked up for me, don't you understand? That's what I'm trying to tell you. You can never, ever be too fucked up for me, no matter what's hiding deep down inside of you—so stop being afraid to show me everything. I'm telling you to let your freak flag fly loud and proud. I'm telling you I won't run away. I won't reject you. You can trust me." Tears pour out of my eyes. I'm in danger of losing myself to a *bona fide* ugly cry.

His relief is palpable. He kisses me. "Don't leave me."

I snort. "I'm not going anywhere. You're the one who's the flight risk."

His lips are on mine. His tongue is in my mouth. Even if my brain wanted to leave this man, my body would stage a coup. Tears blur my eyes and run down my cheeks. "I just don't understand why you hold back like you do. I'm giving you everything, Jonas. I want the same from you."

"I can't," he whispers.

"Yes, you can."

He shakes his head. "This is all because I wouldn't stay tied up? I don't understand—what happened after you untied me was incredible."

"It's a *metaphor*, Jonas. Come on. I know how you love your metaphors."

"I know it was a metaphor. I'm not stupid. But maybe we enacted a different and even better metaphor than the one you were going for. Sometimes, the best things are unplanned."

"No, I'm pretty sure a better metaphor is not what just happened—I want *my* metaphor, Jonas, and what I just discovered is that it's just not possible for you." I huff out an exasperated puff of air. "You ready for another Plato quote, hmm? I've become somewhat of a Plato aficionado lately."

His gaze is steady.

"'You can discover more about a person in an hour of play than in a year of conversation.'"

He squints at me.

"And I just discovered a lot."

He glares at me.

"You don't like having Plato used against you?"

Oh boy, he's not happy with me.

"I wanted you to take a leap of faith the way I did when I jumped thirty feet into blackness. And you couldn't do it. Clearly."

He smashes his lips together. "You don't understand."

"Only because you won't explain it to me!"

He's about to lose it. "Why are you doing this? Who cares *why* I didn't want to be tied up. You untied me and we moved forward and it was fucking amazing. We don't have to talk about every goddamned thing we *feel* all the time, do we?"

"Jonas," I sigh. "I know you're not familiar with the practice, but what we're doing right now is this really weird thing adults do sometimes. It's called talking about our feelings. It's okay. We'll survive it, I promise." What was that psychobabble quote Josh used when they disagreed the other day? Oh yes. "*Talking* about it doesn't mean we're *disagreeing*."

"Oh good God, please don't say that. You know not what you do."

I smile and touch his cheek.

He rubs his eyes. "You just don't understand."

"Then tell me."

He's silent.

"This whole time, you've been acting like you're some Kung Fu master and I'm your little Grasshopper in desperate need of enlightenment. But, ironically, here we are: I've surrendered to you mind, body and soul—in every way a woman can surrender to a man, sometimes against my natural instincts—and it's *you* who's holding back on *me*. I can *feel* it. And the closer and closer I feel to you, the more my heart opens and opens and bleeds—the more I start to *need* you—it scares me. It's just starting to feel like there's this gaping void between us that's eventually going to swallow me up and crush my heart into a million tiny pieces."

I'm panting. That speech took a lot out of me.

He rubs his hands over his face. "I told Josh I'm quitting Faraday & Sons. I told him right before I came into the bedroom."

"Oh, Jonas, that's amazing news." I don't understand the connection between this revelation and what we've been talking about, but I'm sure it's coming. I wait.

He waits a long beat and finally speaks again. "I can finally envision the life I want. I see it. I finally know exactly what it looks like."

"That's so good."

"For the first time in my life, I can finally, clearly visualize the divine original form of Jonas Faraday. I've tried to visualize the divine original of myself for so long, Sarah, and I couldn't see him. Or, on my best days, I could sort of see him—but he was blurry or dark or flickering in and out. But now, he's finally crystal clear."

I wait, my pulse pounding in my ears.

His breathing is shaky. "I can see him right in front of me, Sarah." He swallows hard. "He's standing next to you, holding your hand."

My heart leaps. Oh. My. God.

"I can finally see him because you grabbed his hand and guided him into the light."

There are no words.

He stifles a soft yelping noise. "Every heart sings a song, incomplete, until another heart whispers back." His voice brims with emotion. "My song is now complete."

Oh, holy Baby Jesus in a manger.

The time for thinking is done. My brain can go to hell. My body wants to go to heaven. I grab his face and kiss him deeply and then make love to him tenderly until we both fall soundly asleep in each other's arms.

Chapter 21
Jonas

I sit at the kitchen table drafting the press release announcing my departure from Faraday & Sons. Each word I type brings me closer to the man I'm meant to be—the divine original form of Jonas Faraday. Genuine happiness is within my grasp.

Sarah enters the kitchen. She's showered and dressed and ready to kick some ass, as usual. She's got her laptop tucked under her arm and a book bag over her shoulder.

"Good morning, beautiful. Can I make you an omelet?"

"We need to talk," she says.

Not my favorite phrase. No pleasant conversation with any woman throughout history has ever started with those words.

"You wanna talk about your Maltese Kiki?" I ask hopefully.

"No," she answers, unsmiling. She sits down at the table.

I'm filled with unease. My stomach flip-flops.

"I need to stay at my place for a few days, just so I can study and get back on track—"

"No fucking way."

"Excuse me?" she says, her cheeks instantly turning red.

"No fucking way. First of all, I want you here with me, as you know, so I can ravage you at a moment's notice, any time of day. But second of all, and more importantly, it's not safe. I don't want you to be alone for a single minute until we hear from The Club and get a read on how this is whole thing's gonna shake out."

"Well, that's just crazy. What if we never hear from them? What if they trashed my place and took my computer and that's the last we're ever gonna hear from them?"

"I highly doubt it."

165

"I have a hunch you're wrong."

I let out a long, controlled exhale. This woman is such a pain in the ass, I swear to God. "Let's just say for the sake of argument your hunch is right and we don't hear from them. You're comfortable relying on their silence as some sort of tacit truce? You'll be able to sleep at night—no looking over your shoulder, no wondering if they're coming for you?"

She purses her lips, giving the matter due consideration.

"And what happened to defending all the poor saps who joined The Club looking for true love?"

"I've been thinking a lot about that, during the approximately seven minutes I haven't been having sex with you since we got back from our trip."

I laugh.

"I think I might have been naïve about that. Maybe that software engineer guy was the exception, not the rule, and the vast majority of guys who join The Club want to ride a Mickey Mouse roller coaster, just like Josh said. Maybe they don't care, or even want to know, how The Club supplies the fantasy."

I blink fast a couple times, trying to process what she's saying. "So you're saying if they were to leave you alone, you'd really just leave them alone? Live and let live?"

She shrugs. "Yeah, I think the message I gave to Stacy was honest—if they leave me alone, I'll leave them alone. The only part I lied about was having that report. Oh, and mentioning the Secret Service, too, that was just a total bluff. I've never seen their membership roster."

"Utter brilliance."

"Thank you." She sighs. "But, yeah, I've thought about it, and I'm not sure I care enough to make this the center of my universe. I've got a life to live—things I care a helluva lot more about than taking down a prostitution ring. And, anyway, if ninety-nine percent of The Club's members wouldn't want to know the truth, who am I to ruin the fantasy for them?"

I stare at her for a long time. "Wow. I never thought I'd see the day."

"What?"

"Your Hallmark-Lifetime brainwashing has finally succumbed to cynicism and realism. So you don't believe in fairytales anymore?"

"Oh, I still believe in fairytales, now more than ever." She levels a smoldering gaze at me that makes my heart explode. "It's just that I realized something really important about fairytales."

I wait.

"You can't take them for granted. They're precious. Rare. If you're one of the lucky few who gets to live a fairytale, you best spend your time and energy cherishing it, reveling in it, holding onto it—as opposed to, say, running around trying to take down an Internet sex club." She gives me a look that makes me want to drop to my knees.

My heart is an old, stiff sponge, long neglected on a sink ledge, and it's just been dunked into a warm bucket of water. I get up from the table and walk toward her, my heart-sponge absorbing and enlarging and dripping its bounty with each step. I take her in my arms and kiss every inch of her face and she trembles with the pleasure of it. I take her face in my hands and kiss her mouth and she audibly swoons.

This is one of the top ten moments of my entire life. My baby just called me her Prince Charming.

She traces my lips with her fingertip and then kisses me softly.

It takes a moment before my vocal chords work again. "But what if my gut is right, Sarah? What if they're coming for you?"

"I guess I'll just have to take my chances."

I hug her to me. "I'm not willing to do that. I've got to do whatever's necessary to keep you safe."

She exhales. "What are you gonna do, huh? Go to class with me every day for the next two years, just in case?"

"If necessary, yes."

"Well that's not creepy-intense or anything."

We stare at each other, at an impasse.

"Jonas," she says. "Sweet Jonas. I'm going crazy. I haven't had a minute to myself. I have to study. I have to concentrate. I need to get my hair trimmed. I need to go to yoga. And maybe a facial would be nice, too."

I smile.

"I just need a little space. This has all happened so fast—and, baby, you're really *intense,* no offense—I just need a little elbow room."

"Wait a minute—I'm *intense?*" I glare at her with my best Charles Manson eyes.

She laughs. "I need time to study. Remember all that delicious anticipation before Belize? It was hot. Time apart can be a very good thing."

I grab her hand and pull her back to the kitchen table. She sits on my lap.

"Listen to me. If it weren't for this whole thing with The Club, I'd be semi-normal about time apart. You need time to study? Okay. You want to go to yoga and hang out with Kat? Whatever. I like my alone time, too, believe it or not. All of that's normal. But put that shit aside. These aren't normal circumstances, okay? *It's not safe.* I don't want you to be alone until we have a definitive end to all this. That guy who followed you to your class and then showed up at the library wasn't there to sell you Girl Scout cookies."

She rolls her eyes.

"What? Why did you do that?"

"Do what?"

"Roll your eyes."

She doesn't reply.

"What?"

She's quiet.

"You don't believe I saw him?"

She's still quiet.

"You think I just *hallucinated* him?"

She flashes me an if-the-shoe-fits look.

"You think I'm crazy?" I ask softly, the hairs on my arms standing on end. My stomach twists even as I say those words.

"No, I don't think you're crazy, you big dummy. I think you're overprotective and hypersensitive in this particular circumstance, given what you've been through in your life. I think your mind is playing tricks on you."

"Are you fucking kidding me right now?" I make a sound somewhere between a grunt and a howl. "I can take that shit from Josh, but not from you. I thought you understood what I'm trying to do here—I thought we were on the same page."

She laughs. "It's kinda hard to be on the same page when you don't share your strategy with me."

168

I make an exasperated sound. "Would you just let it rest already with that? Jesus. It was a good strategy and I was just trying to protect you. I thought you might try to hijack things—which you *did*, by the way."

"And thank God I did. From where I was standing, your strategy looked pretty effing lame."

"How would you know? You were peeking through a window. And for your information, it was an excellent strategy. Stacy was just about to give me her boss's email address when you barged in."

"Oh, really?"

"Yes, really. And then you waltzed in and... yes, you made my strategy look like child's play compared to yours because you're a fucking genius—damn, baby, you were magnificent, you know that? So sexy. You slayed me." I shake it off. "But the point is I was just about to get the information I wanted when you came in and—surprise, surprise—hijacked everything with your never-ending bossiness."

"You are so fucking hot, do you know that, Jonas Faraday?"

My cock tingles.

She smiles at me. "Tell me everything Stacy said before I came in."

I tell her every last thing I can remember from our conversation. Sarah's wheels are turning. God help us all, she's *thinking*.

"Well, then," she finally says. "It's obvious what we need to do. Let's go talk to Oksana the Ukrainian in Las Vegas. I'm not gonna just sit around, letting my boyfriend follow me to law school every day, waiting for The Club to contact me. I'm gonna write a kick-ass report that'll scare the bajeezus out of them and then I'm gonna hand-deliver it to Oksana the Ukrainian Pimpstress personally. Big risk, big reward, right, Jonas? Isn't that what Professor Faraday preached to my contracts class?"

"In *business*, Sarah. Not with you. I can't afford to take any risk, big or small, when it comes to you."

"Well, I can and will and you can't stop me." She smiles like she's a kid taunting me on a playground. "It's a free country," she adds, just for good measure. "And anyway, don't you have plenty of stuff to do? Like quitting your big, important mogul-job or running your new gyms or getting that flabby body of yours into shape or climbing a rock?"

169

I sigh. "I don't even have an address for Oksana. Stacy said she's just got a P.O. box. I was just about to get Oksana's email address, but thanks to my bossy girlfriend's impeccable timing, we've got no way to contact her."

"Oh, Silly Rabbit, Trix are for kids. We've already got everything we need to find Oksana."

"We do?"

"Of course, we do, rookie. Leave it to me." She looks at her watch. "And in the meantime, I've got a constitutional law class to attend—*alone*." She gets up from the table. "Oh, and by the way, to keep you company over the next couple days of our Delicious Anticipation 2.0, I made you a playlist—a little mix tape, from me to you." She tosses a flash drive onto the table. "Tit for tat, baby." She winks and turns toward the front door.

"Sarah."

She stops and faces me.

"Sorry to make you waste such a witty exit—'tit for tat, baby'— mmm, it was sassy, clever, and flirty—everything I adore about you—the American judge rates it a perfect ten—but you can forget about walking out that door by yourself. No fucking way."

She groans and sits back down at the table. She opens her laptop.

"What are you doing?"

"Saving my sanity." She clicks into her emails. "I'm gonna lob a Hail Mary." She squints at her screen and begins typing. "Member Services at the club dot com," she says as she types. "That's the only email address I've got for them."

"What email address did they use to send applications to you?"

"All applications and intake reports were delivered back and forth through a drop box." She twists her mouth thinking for a moment. "Maybe your hacker could try to trace that?"

"Good idea. I don't really know how that works."

"Neither do I, but let's ask him."

"Okay."

She looks back at her screen. "I'll keep my email pretty vague— you never know who's going to be on the receiving end of it or whether it might be confiscated down the line by authorities one day. Although, come to think of it, I'm already probably screwed if that ever happens." She sighs. "I'll just keep my cards close to my vest and say just enough to entice them to contact me." She types, rapidly mouthing the words as she goes. "There. I told them I have something urgent to talk to them about—something they're definitely going to want to hear—and to please contact me right away." She clicks her tongue. "Okay. Plan A is to locate Oksana and scare the bajeezus out of her, face-to-face—never underestimate the power of in-person communication. But in the meantime, I'll send this email and cross my fingers they reply. I'm not gonna just sit around and hope something happens—I'm gonna *make* it happen."

"Shocker."

She shrugs. "I've got to do something, Jonas. If every day for the next two years is gonna be Take Your Hot Boyfriend to Class Day, I'm gonna have a frickin' nervous breakdown."

Chapter 22
Sarah

"Can't you maybe just sit in the back of the class and pretend you don't know me? Or at least try not to be so Jonas-y?"

"What does that even mean?"

"It means you don't exactly *blend*."

"Really? You really want me to sit in the back of the class?"

"Yeah, I really do. This is just so totally weird. I won't be able to concentrate on what the professor says if you're sitting next to me making me all hot and bothered. And I guarantee half the class won't be able to concentrate, either. You're just so... Jonas-y."

"Stop saying that. I have no idea what you're talking about."

"False modesty doesn't become you."

He rolls his eyes. "Okay, I'll sit in the back when class starts, okay? I've got plenty to do on my laptop, anyway—some numbers to crunch about the various gym locations. But am I allowed to sit here with you until class starts?"

I look at my watch. "Yeah. We've still got plenty of time. But when the classroom starts to fill up, you best scoot your delectable ass to the back, big boy."

He pouts. "Okay."

"Aw, poor Jonas with the sad eyes."

"I'll survive."

"You know, you could hire a professional bodyguard for me if you're really this worried. Problem solved. Then you could live your life again, and I could live mine, and we could attack each other like animals at home all night long like a normal couple."

"I like hearing you say that."

"Attack each other like animals?" I shoot him a wicked grin.

172

"Well, yes. But that's not what I meant." He smiles.

"Like a normal couple?"

"No—and, by the way, I don't think most normal couples attack each other like animals."

I try to remember what I just said. "All night long." I smile broadly.

"Nope."

I'm stumped. What else did I say?

"*Home.*" He smiles shyly. Fourth grader Jonas has made yet another appearance on the playground. "I like hearing you call my house your home."

We share a googly-eyed, infatuated smile.

"You're a diehard romantic, you know that?" I say.

"Shh. Not so loud."

"Mum's the word."

He pauses. "So you'd be okay with me hiring a bodyguard for you?"

"No, I'd be mortified. But I bet I could give a bodyguard the slip way easier than I could ditch your paranoid ass—I sure ditched Josh in record time."

"Okay, so much for that idea. Speaking of which, have you spoken to Kat? How's the bodyguard working out for her?"

"It seems her bodyguard is extremely attentive."

He rolls his eyes. "You're telling me I'm paying some guy to screw Kat?"

"Ew, Jonas, no. They're not having sex. Give Kat some credit."

He smirks at me.

"Well, okay, yes. She'd probably have sex with him, but the guy's a professional. Sex with the client is against the Bodyguard Code, isn't it? At least that's what Kevin Costner said in the movie."

"Yeah, right before he slept with Whitney Houston."

"Oh yeah, I forgot about that part. But, anyway, never mind. All I meant was the guy's not at all bummed about his assignment." I laugh. "He should just get in line—it's the way everyone reacts to Kat."

He laughs. "Yeah, Josh was pretty intrigued."

"Really? Aw."

"What did Kat think of Josh?"

173

"She thought he was... a little Douche-y McDouchey-pants, to be honest."

Jonas looks disappointed.

"Sorry. I think it was the Mickey Mouse roller coaster thing that rubbed her the wrong way."

"No doubt."

"But I reminded her that you were a cocky-asshole-motherfucker when I first met you, so you never know."

"Aw, how sweet."

"So how long are you planning to keep paying that guy to watch Kat, anyway?"

"I don't know. I hadn't given it much thought. However long it's necessary, I guess."

I consider his beautiful face for a moment, the earnest expression on it. The kindness in his eyes. "You're so thoughtful, you know that? You say you're not a natural to wear a red cape, but I think you sell yourself short."

He twists his mouth. "Thank you." He blushes.

Oh good Lord, this boy slays me.

We stare at each other for a long beat. I don't know what he's thinking, but I'm sure as hell thinking, *I love you.*

"If you were Josh, I'd have to slap my face right now," he finally says.

"What?" I laugh.

"Never mind."

I look at my watch. Twelve minutes before the start of class. I'd better get my head in the game.

"Okay, chitchat time over," I bark. "I've gotta get crunked."

He laughs. "Do your thing, baby."

I go through my pre-class ritual. I put a bottle of water on my desk. I open my laptop and open a new blank document. I pull out my textbook, a spiral notebook, and a ballpoint pen from my book bag. (In case anything goes wrong with my computer, I always like to have a good old-fashioned pen and paper handy during class.) I begin writing today's date at the top of my notebook page, but my ballpoint pen doesn't work. Dang it. I rummage into my purse for another one... and discover an envelope. I pull it out, perplexed. Where did this come from? I open it. Inside, there's a check made payable to me in the amount of two hundred fifty thousand dollars from one Jonas P. Faraday. I can't breathe. I keep looking from "Sarah Cruz" to "two hundred fifty thousand dollars and no cents." My brain can't process what my eyes are seeing.

My head swivels to look at Jonas.

He's engrossed in something on his laptop, totally oblivious to what I'm holding in my hand.

"Jonas." I hold up the check with a shaky hand.

He glances over at me. His cheeks burst with sudden color.

"Jonas," I say again. "I can't. What . . .?"

I've never held this much money in my hand in all my life. I'm trembling. I can't believe he did this.

"I didn't intend for you to find that right now," he says.

"Jonas," I say yet again, my vocabulary apparently having been reduced to the developmental level of a toddler's. "No." I can't accept this from him—but I'm electrified that he wanted to do it for me.

"Let me explain my thinking on this," he begins.

"I couldn't possibly accept—"

"Just hear me out, Sarah."

My mouth hangs open. This is crazy.

"You were right. Anything could happen in the next six months. You could decide I'm too fucked up for you, after all. You could get bored with me. You could decide I don't give you enough space... or that I'm not able to express my feelings the way you need me to... Or that I'm too intense." He swallows hard. "Anything could happen. But no matter what might happen between us, I want to make your dreams come true, regardless—even if it turns out I'm not destined to be a part of them.

"So this money is yours, Sarah, whether or not you wind up winning that scholarship, whether or not you wind up wanting to be with me. Put it in your bank account. It's yours from this moment forward, no strings attached. If you get the scholarship and don't need the money for school, then use it for something else that will make your life easier. Donate it to your mom's charity, whatever. But if you don't get the scholarship, then use it to pay for your schooling. Given who you are and what you plan to do when you graduate, this money will ultimately wind up making the world a better place, either way."

I burst into tears.

"Don't cry. I did it to make you smile—not to make you *cry*."

I can't speak. I'm too overwhelmed with emotion.

"Oh, baby, don't cry."

It's several minutes before I can carry on a coherent conversation.

"But why so much?" I ask. "It's so much money, Jonas—too much. Even if I were going to accept tuition from you, which I'm not saying I'm going to do, I could never, ever accept this. This is crazy."

"Well, now, think about it for a minute. You've got student loans for this first year, right?"

I nod.

"And then you've got tuition for years two and three, if the scholarship doesn't pan out. Plus, you'll have to pay taxes on the money—and trust me, taxes are a bitch. You'll be shocked about how much of this will go to Uncle Sam."

I wipe my eyes, shaking.

"It's really not an excessive amount, considering all that."

I'm speechless.

He reaches over to me and strokes a lock of my hair. "I didn't pick that amount at random, Sarah." He flashes me mournful eyes. "It's my penance."

I shake my head. He owes me nothing—least of all penance. When I whispered into his ear about his "penance" last night in bed, I was just being naughty. This man owes no penance to anyone, least of all to me.

"I'm ashamed I was willing to pay that ridiculous sum to feed my demons. Maybe this small gesture will help balance out my karmic ledger somehow. Or, at least, help me clear my conscience."

Tears gush out of my eyes.

"Good actions give strength to ourselves and inspire good actions in others," he says.

I grin through my tears. "Plato?"

"Plato."

I take a deep, shaky, tearful breath. "Thank you so much, Jonas. There are no words to describe how grateful I am. You're a beautiful person, inside and out. But—"

"No but. Please. Just say yes. Just once in your goddamned life do what I want you to do, woman." His voice is tender. "Please. I beg you, don't be a pain in the ass this time. I need to do this."

176

I'm gaping like a fish on a line. This money would change my life, there's no question about it. But it's just too much to accept. I look into his eyes, perhaps searching for a sign—something to guide me in my decision-making—and I see love in his eyes. Pure, unadulterated and unconditional love.

"Jonas," I whisper, my head swirling.

"Sarah, I *insist*," he says, softly. And then he graces me with his most dazzling Jonas Faraday smile.

I laugh despite my tears. What mortal could possibly resist this man?

"Oh, well, if you *insist*," I say.

He smiles.

I shake my head. "Just give me tonight to sleep on it," I say. I put the check back into my purse. "It's just so much money." I put my hand on his cheek. "My sweet Jonas."

I lean forward to kiss him. His lips are magical. I love him with all my heart and soul. I don't know what secrets and pain he continues to harbor deep inside himself, and I don't care—whatever it is, we'll excavate it together. However long it takes, however slowly he needs to go, we'll take it one step at a time. We've got all the time in the world, after all. I'm not going anywhere. I wipe my eyes and my fingers come away blackened with mascara.

"Oh, jeez," I say. "Tell me the truth—does my face looks like the BP oil spill right now?"

He laughs. "No, not at all. You look beautiful."

"I'll be right back." I stand.

Jonas stands, too. "I'll come with you."

"Oh my God, Jonas. The restroom is literally right outside the door—right on the other side of the hallway. Relax. I'll pop in there, pee really fast, wash my face, blow my nose, and come right back here in record time. I promise. I'll be greased lightning. Sit down." I grab my purse, just in case I want to reapply a little mascara after I clean myself up.

He vacillates.

I throw up my hands. "You can't come into the women's restroom with me, Jonas. This is a college campus. They'll put up posters warning students there's a crazy bathroom stalker on the loose. Come on, babe. I know you're paranoid, but please try not to be *crazy* paranoid."

He sighs. "Hang on."

I watch as he strides to the back of the classroom, pokes his head out the door, looks up and down the hallway five or six times, and comes back.

"Okay. All clear." He grins. "I can never be too careful when it comes to protecting my precious baby."

I roll my eyes. "I'll be right back." I kiss the top of his head. "And when I come back, I want you to move to the back of the classroom, okay? This whole I-can't-go-anywhere-without-my-hot-boyfriend thing is starting to embarrass me."

Chapter 23
Sarah

"Oh jeez," I mutter aloud, looking at myself in the bathroom mirror. Despite what Jonas said, my face does, in fact, look like an oil slick.

That check from Jonas really threw me for a loop. I can't remember the last time geysers spontaneously shot out of my eyes like that. It was like I'd been crowned Miss America, received a marriage proposal, given birth to quintuplets, and won the power ball lottery all at once. I've got so many emotions bouncing around inside my body right now, I can't think straight. The only coherent thought I can muster is, "I love you, Jonas," over and over. Damn, that boy is a dream come true.

I turn on the faucet and splash cold water onto my eyes and scrub the errant mascara off my face. I grab a paper towel and wipe my face dry and then blow my runny nose. I'm a train wreck. A mushy pile of goo. The luckiest girl in the world.

I pull a tube of lip gloss out of my purse and apply a little shimmer to my lips. Meh, I think I'll skip reapplying mascara—at the rate I'm going, I'm sure that wasn't my last good cry of the day.

I head into one of two empty stalls, lock the stall door, and sit down to pee.

I hear the bathroom door open. Footsteps enter the room and stop. No one enters the empty stall next to me. That's weird. Whoever she is, why is she waiting on my stall when there's an empty one?

I bend over to peek underneath the partition, but I can't see all the way to the door from this angle. I'd have to get down on my hands and knees to see that far. But there's definitely another human being in this bathroom with me. I wait. No more footsteps. Why is my bathroom buddy standing just inside the door? Did she stop to look for a tampon in her purse? Or is my stealthy bathroom visitor my gorgeous but highly paranoid boyfriend checking up on me?

"Jonas?"

There's no reply.

"If that's you, wait for me outside, you creeper-weirdo."

I hear the lock on the bathroom door click.

"Jonas?" I'm suddenly uneasy. "Is there someone there?"

It's got to be Jonas. Is he sneaking in here for a quickie— inspired by our bathroom escapades last night? I roll my eyes. That was a one-off. I'm not planning to make bathroom-sex a habit. And, anyway, we can't do it right now—class starts in five minutes. Although who am I kidding?—with the right persuasion, Jonas Faraday could convince me to have sex with him anywhere, anytime, even in a gross bathroom stall five minutes before class.

The footsteps walk slowly toward the stall.

My chest constricts. I swallow hard. Those footsteps don't sound like a woman. And they're definitely not Jonas' footsteps, either. That's a shuffle. Jonas doesn't shuffle. Jonas is grace in motion. I pull up my jeans and flush the toilet, my blood pulsing in my ears. I clutch my purse and open the stall door.

Holy shit. It's John Fucking Travolta from *Pulp Fiction*, ponytail and all. A small knife glints unmistakably in his hand. I'm too terrified to make a sound or move a muscle.

In a flash, he yanks me out of the stall by my T-shirt. The knife glints as his hand moves toward my neck.

"Oksana!" I scream. "Oksana!"

He's intrigued enough to pause. He presses the knife into my throat.

But he doesn't slice.

"You're supposed to talk to Oksana," I blurt. "You have new instructions from Oksana!"

A terrified squeal rises up out of me. I try to suppress it, but I can't. I'm a quivering mess. My knees buckle, but he holds me up, holding the knife roughly against my neck. Good thing I just peed, or else I'd surely wet my pants.

"You know Oksana?" He has a thick accent of some kind.

"Yes, Oksana—the Crazy Ukrainian." I try to smirk conspiratorially, but I'm sure I just look like I'm having a seizure.

He's not amused. Oh shit. Maybe he's Ukrainian, too. "Oksana in Las Vegas—at headquarters. She has new instructions for you. You're not supposed to hurt me. Things have changed—Oksana will tell you."

"My instruction is to kill you." His eyes are hard.

At this last statement, my knees go weak. He grabs me and holds me up, still holding the knife firmly against my throat—but, still, he's not slicing.

I keep babbling like my life depends on it—because, surely, it does.

"You were supposed to get new instructions last night or this morning. No kill." In my terror, those last two words come out like I'm talking to Koko, the sign language gorilla.

He stares at me blankly, pressing the knife into my neck.

Oh shit, he's got no effing idea what I'm talking about. Stacy hasn't conveyed last night's message to anyone yet—or, if she has, word hasn't made its way up (or down) the totem pole to this guy. He's pressing the knife so hard against my throat, the blade is breaking the skin. My skin under the knife burns.

He grits his teeth and his eyes flash like he's made a decision—and not a good one.

"Two-hundred-fifty-thousand dollars!" I scream.

He pauses yet again, just long enough for me to keep talking.

"Right here in my purse. From the rich guy. Two hundred fifty thousand dollars! Look in my purse. You can have it. And I can get you more."

He pauses briefly, processing what I'm saying, and then puts me in a suffocating headlock while he gruffly opens my purse. He pulls out the check, grunting with pleasure or surprise or malice, I'm not sure which.

"I've been scamming the rich guy all along. He gave me this money, and there's plenty more where that came from. I just sent The Club an email about this earlier today. I want to be partners with you. That's why I emailed you. Call your boss, you'll see. I sent an email. I'm scamming this guy—and I can do the same thing to other new members, too. We can make money together. Lots of money." I'm panting. I'm light-headed.

He holds up the check and leans into my face. "You can get more?"

Oh God, his breath is foul.

"Yeah, lots more—lots and lots and lots and lots and lots." Oh God, I'm rambling. "And not just from him. I can get it from other guys, too. I'll split everything with you. That's what I emailed about this morning—ask them about my email, you'll see. This guy paid his membership fee and now he only wants to fuck me—he wants a GFE . . ." I mentally say a prayer of gratitude to Stacy the Faker for providing this helpful bit of prostitute lingo. "These kinds of guys love a good GFE. They think I'm breaking the rules to be with them—we're Romeo and Juliet. We can do this with all the new members. I'll tell them a sob story about my law school tuition and throw in a sick mom with cancer and they'll fork over big money to feel like my knight in shining armor. We'll split the money."

He's considering. Or, at least, he's not killing me yet.

"I'm not gonna tell anyone about The Club—why would I do that? That's the last thing I want to do. This is my ticket to big money. I love what you're doing to these rich assholes—I want in. Let me be your partner. I'll give these guys the Intake Agent GFE before they ever start using the other girls. I'm the girl they're not supposed to have, the forbidden fruit. This first stupid guy gave me two hundred fifty thousand bucks—and I can get lots more. Call your boss—ask if I emailed this morning like I'm telling you. You'll see—I'm telling the truth. Call and find out. I sent an email this morning."

I'm going to faint. I can't keep talking like this. I'm seeing spots. My chest is jerking and jolting from the exertion of trying to take air into my lungs and speak at the same time. I've never felt so much adrenaline coursing through my veins in all my life. There is no doubt in my mind this man is a heartbeat away from plunging that knife into my chest. I'm shaking.

"Call your boss. Come on, Hugo."

He scrunches his face, amused. It's the first flicker of humanity I've seen from him during this whole exchange. I take it as a positive sign.

"What? Don't tell me Hugo's not your name? Oh man! And you look like such a Hugo, too."

One side of his mouth hitches up.

"When we start working together, I'm gonna call you Hugo. That'll be my pet name for you. You'll always be my Hugo." I smile at him. Or, at least, I try to. I'm sure my face looks more like a raccoon caught in headlights.

He looks at the check in his hand. "You can get more?"

"Much more. I put on a big show last night when the rich guy was at a check-in with Stacy. He *loved* it. Fucked my brains out in the bathroom afterwards and gave me the money. We can do that kind of thing all the time to new members." I try to laugh. "These guys love a good GFE—they're all just diehard romantics underneath it all. Go on—call your boss. Ask about my email this morning. You'll see."

My breathing is fitful. Sweat has broken out over my brow.

Without warning, he puts me into a headlock again, smashing my face against his body, and pulls out his phone. I can't see what he's doing, but I hear the condensed sound of an automated outgoing voicemail message followed by a beep. He leaves a gruff, staccato message in another language. Russian?

I'm going to die at the hands of a James Bond villain.

He yanks me back up by my hair and presses the knife into my throat even harder than before. I feel blood trickling down my neck. My skin is on fire.

His nostrils flare. He jerks his face right into my mine and I squeal, flinching, certain this is it for me—but he holds up the check.

"If you're lying to me, I'll come back and slit your throat."

My neck burns sharply as he lets go of my quivering body—did he just nick me with the knife? Just as I bring my hand up to my neck, a shocking pain in my ribcage burns hotter and fiercer than anything I've felt in my entire life. The intense pain makes my knees buckle and takes my breath away, literally. My legs give way. As I fall, the bathroom spins and twists before my eyes.

A crashing jolt of pain slams the back of my head.

I love you, Jonas.

Darkness.

Chapter 24
Jonas

I move to the back of the classroom, just as she instructed. I'm Sarah's puppy dog, after all—a fucking Maltese named Jonas. Sit, stay, come. Whatever the hell she wants me to do, I'll do it.

The classroom's almost full. A guy takes the seat I just vacated, the one right next to hers. I glance at her open laptop and notebook on her empty desk and feel a pang of envy. I want to be the one who gets to sit next to her—damn, I shouldn't have moved.

I look at my watch. Still a couple minutes before class starts. She'd better hurry the fuck up. What's she doing in there all this time? Putting makeup on? If so, I wish she wouldn't. She doesn't need it.

The professor enters the room and heads down the aisle toward the front of the class. Before he makes it to his destination, a student stops him to ask a question.

I reach into my jeans pocket and fish out the flash drive she gave me this morning. Let's see what songs my baby's compiled for my mix tape. I've never gotten a playlist from a girl before, ever, and I have to admit, I'm excited about it.

I reach into my computer case for some earbuds and shove them into my ears.

The first song is "Demons" by Imagine Dragons. I smile. Oh, Sarah, aren't you clever? I get it. I've got demons and you're going to save me from them. I don't need to listen to this song—I've heard it a million times.

The next song is "Not Afraid" by Eminem. I'm sensing a theme here. This woman is bound and determined to "heal" me, huh? I guess I'd better get used to it. It's just the way she's wired.

"Come a Little Closer" by Cage the Elephant. I'm not familiar with this one. I listen to the song for about thirty seconds, through the end of the first chorus. Love the song. And, yes, definitely a theme. She wants me to "come a little closer"—or, as my various past girlfriends have fruitlessly demanded, to "let her in." Not very original, but surely heartfelt.

The professor moves to the podium at the front of the class and organizes his notes. I look at my watch. She's got maybe another minute, if she's lucky. If she doesn't come in the next thirty seconds, I'll knock at the restroom door and tell her to get her butt in gear. She's so anal about not missing even a minute of class—she made us get here twenty minutes early, for Christ's sake—I'm surprised she's taking so damned long.

I change the page view on my screen so I can see the rest of her selected song titles all at once. My heart explodes. The remainder of her song list forges a decidedly different theme than her initial "let me save you from your demons" campaign: "She Loves You" by the Beatles. "Crazy In Love" by Beyoncé. "Love Don't Cost a Thing" by Jennifer Lopez. "I Just Can't Stop Loving You" by Michael Jackson. And on and on and on. "Love Can Build a Bridge." "All You Need Is Love." "(I Can't Help) Falling In Love With You."

Oh my God.

I bolt out of my chair to a manic stand, wringing my hands, hopping from foot to foot. I need to touch her, kiss her, make love to her. Maybe I'll sneak into that bathroom right now and take her in the stall—no, what am I thinking? We can't have bathroom sex at a time like this. Oh my God. She loves me. We've already told each other this, of course, in oh so many clever and coded ways, but seeing the actual magic word over and over and over on my screen, so starkly, so honestly, so unequivocally—an explicit love letter from my baby to me—it's the greatest feeling in the whole world.

Love is the joy of the good, the wonder of the wise, the amazement of the gods.

"Good morning," the professor begins. "Let's start with the landmark U.S. Supreme Court case of *Lawrence v. Texas* on page one eighty-three of your casebook. Miss Fanuel, will you tell us the holding of this case, please?"

Where the fuck is she? Why is she taking so long?

"Yes. The Supreme Court in *Lawrence v. Texas* held that intimate consensual sexual conduct is part of the liberty protected by the Fourteenth Amendment . . ."

Where is she?

Panic seizes me. She should have come back by now. Holy shit.

She should have come back by now.

Someone screams just outside the classroom door. I bolt out of the room.

A panicked gathering of students stands outside the women's restroom.

"Call 9-1-1!" someone shouts.

I push my way through them into the bathroom.

Blood. Oh my God, no, there's so much blood. It's all over the white tile floor. No, God, please, not again. No more blood. Not again.

I see her bound and bloodied body. The bed sheet is stained a deep, dark red.

I see his brain splattered against the wall. And the floor. And the ceiling. The carpet is stained a deep, dark red.

And now I see my Sarah, My Magnificent Sarah, in a bloodied, crumpled heap, the bracelet I gave her still tied to her lifeless wrist. The white tiles are turning a deep, dark red.

"Call an ambulance!" I scream.

"We called one," someone shrieks. "They'll be here any minute."

I grab at my hair. My body convulses. A howl erupts from me and turns into a gut-wrenching heave. I throw up all over the bathroom floor. Someone tries to come to my aid. I shove them away. Someone grabs at me. I push them away and kneel down on the tile floor next to her.

A guy is bent over her chest, listening for a heartbeat.

Another howl. I pull at my hair.

The guy sits up from her chest and nods at a second guy. There's a collective sigh from the crowd. I push the guy away forcibly. *She's mine.* I scoop her lifeless body up in my arms. I touch every inch of her, patting her down, trying to determine the source of the blood.

"You shouldn't move her," the motherfucker says. I hear the words, but I don't understand the meaning of the words.

186

My fingers search frantically and find a hole in her T-shirt, right above her ribcage. I touch the hole. The fabric around it is warm and wet and red.

"Red," I say, my voice cracking. She promised to stop if I said red. "Red," I choke out again. But it doesn't stop. Make it stop. "Red." My body wracks with sobs as my mind floats above, confounded, detached from my body, spiraling like an airplane smoking and losing altitude.

I pull up her shirt and a strangled cry wrenches from me. A wound. A gaping, red wound in her beautiful olive skin, just like last time—only this time, there's only one angry hole in her flesh instead of too many to count. I put my fingers on the hole to stop the bleeding, just like I did after the big man left. She always said I had magic hands, but she was wrong. There were too many wounds, too many holes to plug, and my fingers were too small. The magic in my hands didn't work that time—no matter how hard I tried.

But this time, there's only one savage hole to plug—and my hands are big. My fingers are strong. The blood stops gurgling out when I cover the wound and press down. This time, the magic in my hands is working. And yet there's still blood coming from somewhere else. Where's the blood still coming from? I look around in panic. There's so much fucking blood, all over the white tile floor. Her neck. Blood is coming from her neck. I put my fingers on the small indentation in her neck and the blood stops flowing.

"Call an ambulance!" I scream. "Call an ambulance!"

"We already called one. They're coming. The hospital's right here on campus. Any minute."

The other guy leans in and puts his fingers on the hole in her ribcage and I cradle her head in my arms, keeping my fingers on her neck.

"Call again!" I scream. I pat my pockets. I can't find my fucking phone. Did I leave it in the fucking classroom? "Call again!" I howl.

I tried to untie the ropes but the knots were too tight—tried to free her wrists, but my fingers weren't strong enough. The magic in my hands didn't work that time, no matter how hard I tried. *I love you,* I said to her, tears bursting out of me. *I love you,* I wailed, willing her to wake up and smile at me again. *I love you, Mommy.* But she wouldn't wake up, no matter how many times I said the magic

187

words. *I love you.* But my love wasn't enough to save her. *Look at me, Mommy.* But her blue eyes stared into space. *Please, Mommy.* Her blue eyes remained frozen. *I love you, Mommy.* But it wasn't enough.

Sarah's blood is all over my jeans, my T-shirt, my arms, my hands. If I could give her my blood, I would. If I could give her my life, I would. Oh God, I'd bleed myself dry for her.

I feel wetness on my forearms. I pull back. My arms are soaked in her blood. My fingers touch the back of her head, the base of her skull—her hair is matted and wet and sticky. I burrow my finger into the wetness and feel an enormous gash.

I howl at my discovery. My body heaves.

The crowd stares at me, paralyzed, wide-eyed, in shock.

I glare at them all, holding my precious baby in my arms.

Heavy footsteps echo in the corridor, getting louder and louder, approaching. I hear the sound of metal wheels.

"At the end!" someone yells in the distant hallway.

I hug her to me.

"Love is the joy of the good, the wonder of the wise, the amazement of the gods," I whimper, but then a dam breaks inside of me and a lifetime of pressure and pain and sorrow and remorse and rage breaks and a fierceness floods into me.

"I love you," I wail, my voice cracking, my gut wrenching, my heart breaking, my mind hurtling into the abyss. "I love you, Sarah. I love you, baby." I shudder with my sobs, rocking her back and forth. I've never felt pain like this. "I love you, baby, I love you, I love you." I look up at the staring crowd. Why are they staring at us? What don't they fucking understand? "I love her," I proclaim fiercely. They stare at me blankly. Why don't these fuckers understand? "I love her," I scream at them all, but they don't understand how I feel. No one ever understands how I feel—except Sarah. Sarah always understands.

I can't lose her. I won't survive it if I lose her. I need them all to understand. Her blood is mine. I'm bleeding all over the floor. I won't survive without her. I need them to understand. I love her.

"I love Sarah Cruz!"

The third book of The Club Trilogy, *The Redemption*, comes out February 9, 2015.

Author Biography

Lauren Rowe is the pen name of an author, performer, audio book narrator, songwriter and media host/personality who decided to unleash her alter ego to write The Club Trilogy to ensure she didn't hold back or self-censor in writing the story. Lauren Rowe lives in San Diego, California where she sings with her band, hosts a show, and writes at all hours of the night. Find out more about The Club Trilogy and Lauren Rowe at www.LaurenRoweBooks.com.

Made in the USA
Middletown, DE
28 January 2015